THE MEDUSA PROJECT

THE RESCUE

Also by Sophie McKenzie

Teen Novels
Girl, Missing
Sister, Missing
Missing Me
Blood Ties
Blood Ransom
Split Second
Every Second Counts

THE MEDUSA PROJECT
The Set-Up
The Hostage
Hunted
Double-Cross
Hit Squad

LUKE AND EVE SERIES
Six Steps to a Girl
Three's a Crowd
The One and Only

FLYNN SERIES
Falling Fast
Burning Bright
Casting Shadows
Defy the Stars

Adult Novels
Close My Eyes
Trust in Me
Here We Lie

THE MEDUSA PROJECT

THE RESCUE

Sophie McKenzie

SIMON & SCHUSTER

Acknowledgements: With thanks to Lou
and Lily Kuenzler and Stephanie Purcell.

First published in Great Britain in 2010 by Simon & Schuster UK Ltd

This edition published in 2021

1 3 5 7 9 10 8 6 4 2

Simon & Schuster UK Ltd
1st Floor, 222 Gray's Inn Road
London
WC1X 8HB

www.simonandschuster.co.uk
www.simonandschuster.com.au
www.simonandschuster.co.in

Simon & Schuster Australia, Sydney
Simon & Schuster India, New Delhi

A CIP catalogue record for this book is available from the British Library.

PB ISBN 978-1-4711-9872-4
eBook ISBN 978-1-84738-892-6

Printed and bound by CPI Group (UK) Ltd, Croydon, CR0 4YY

MIX
Paper from
responsible sources
FSC® C020471

For Aimée, Isabelle and Daniel

Fourteen years ago, scientist William Fox implanted four babies with the Medusa gene – a gene for psychic abilities. Now dead, his experiment left a legacy: four teenagers – Nico, Ketty, Ed and William's own daughter, Dylan – who have each developed their own distinct and special skill.

Brought together by government agent, Geri Paterson, the four make up the Medusa Project – a secret, government-funded, crime-fighting force.

Until recently, the Medusa teens lived under the protection of William's brother, Fergus Fox, at his North London boarding school – Fox Academy. However, their existence has become known to members of the criminal underworld, so they are being taken to a secluded training camp where their identities can be kept secret.

1: ARRIVAL

Spain was unbearably hot. We'd made a pit stop at a roadside café after a solid five-hour drive and, even though it was late afternoon, the sun was still fierce on the back of my head. Everyone else was still inside the café, but I'd come outside for a moment by myself. I was leaning against the car, the metal hot against my back, looking into the distance. All I could see was desert: sand ... rocks ... and, further away, a range of purple-tipped mountains.

The café door banged and Ketty emerged. 'Kind of bleak, isn't it, Ed?' she said as she reached me. 'And way too hot to run in.'

I nodded. Ketty's my best friend – and a keen runner. Like me, she has the Medusa gene but whereas I can read minds, Ketty can predict the future. I glanced at her, trying not to look her in the eye – if I make eye contact with anyone I automatically see into their thoughts and feelings.

You probably think that would be cool.

Trust me, it isn't.

Ketty looked surprisingly unbothered by the heat. She was wearing shorts and a T-shirt. No sweat patches, unlike me, though a couple of her dark brown curls were stuck damply to her forehead.

'Did Geri say how much further?' I asked. Geri Paterson, the head of the Medusa Project, was driving us to a training camp where we were going to have to stay – with no contact with our families – for six whole months.

'Another hour or so.' Ketty sighed.

I shook my head. Everything felt wrong. The journey was long and boring, sure. But I was in no hurry to reach the camp either – the whole point of being sent there, Geri had said, was to 'learn discipline through hard work'. Goodness knows what it would be like, but the thought of it filled me with horror. Physical activities are not exactly my strong point.

Nico emerged from the café to join us. 'Depressed because you won't be going to school for half a year, Ed?' He put his arm round Ketty, a big grin on his face.

Ketty beamed up at him. I turned away. I'm not going into it here, but a few weeks before, she and I dated a bit. Then Nico told her he liked her and now they were all over each other. As Dylan might have said, it sucked *big time*.

Geri strode out of the café. It didn't look as though stopping for a break from driving had improved her mood at all. She was posing as the parent/school liaison officer responsible for taking the four of us to the camp. She jumped into the driver's seat, calling angrily for us to join her.

'Come *on*.'

We sat as before, Nico and Ketty in the back, Dylan on her own in the middle row of seats and me up front next to Geri. I get a bit car sick if I sit anywhere else. Mind you, the next part of our journey was enough to make anyone puke. The road quickly disappeared and we started bumping over really rocky ground. With a snarl, Dylan appeared from behind her oversized sunglasses and took out her headphones.

'When are we going to quit freakin' bouncing around?'

I closed my eyes. Geri was in a bad enough mood without Dylan provoking her further. Geri sucked in her breath. 'May I remind you that if you four hadn't taken matters on your last job into your own hands, then you wouldn't have to be here at all,' she snapped.

Behind me, Ketty sighed. Her brother, Lex, was the reason we'd gone off on our own on our last job. The criminal we were investigating, Damian Foster, had been holding him captive and Ketty had been attempting to find out where he was. The rest of us were helping. I knew Ketty felt responsible for getting us all into trouble with Geri. I turned round and smiled at her. She smiled gratefully back.

'Just because you're sending us to some brat camp doesn't mean it has to be in the middle of nowhere,' Dylan snarled, shoving her headphones back on.

'It's in the middle of nowhere for your own protection,' Geri said. I glanced down at her fists, gripping the steering wheel. She was holding on so tightly that her knuckles were white. 'And may I remind you that I was up for *hours* last

3

night finding a new camp after the original one was compromised.'

The atmosphere in the car chilled further. Geri had reminded us of this fact on average once every ten minutes for the entire journey.

'Yeah, you said,' Nico said sarcastically.

'This is *not* what I signed up for,' Geri muttered. 'I expected you all to behave ... to do what I told you ...'

I looked away. As usual I'd been lumped in with the others. It wasn't fair.

'We didn't sign up for any of this, either,' Nico muttered.

I could hear Ketty whispering in his ear, presumably telling him to calm down. I sighed. Nico was right, of course. None of us had chosen to be part of the Medusa Project – not the original gene implantation before we were born, nor the crime-fighting work we were being trained to do now. Geri was forcing us to work for her.

After another half an hour or so, with the sun hovering over the distant mountains, a long, white building shimmered into view.

'Is that it?' I leaned forward, straining to see the place that was going to be our home from now until October.

'Yes, dear.' The sharp edges of Geri's bob batted her chin as she gave a vigorous nod. 'Camp Felicidad.' She raised her voice. 'Dylan, take those headphones out. I need to go over your final briefing.'

Grumbling, Dylan did so.

'What does Feliss-y-whatsit mean?' Ketty asked.

4

'Camp Happiness,' I translated. 'Hey, maybe the name's a good sign.'

Behind me, Dylan snorted. 'Yeah, right, Chino Boy.'

Dylan was always taking the mickey out of my clothes … out of me generally, in fact. Not that I cared, really.

As we drew nearer, Geri went through our cover stories again. We had each been assigned a new surname and background, part of which was that we'd all attended the same school. I was Ed Jones, bright but lazy – a formerly straight-A student, who was now giving his wealthy parents a massive headache because he wanted to spend his days smoking weed instead of concentrating on his GCSEs.

'Remember, you're all the delinquent children of well-off, middle-class, concerned parents,' Geri cautioned. 'Like everyone else at the camp.'

'Oh good,' Dylan drawled. 'Six months with a bunch of spoilt brats … I can't wait.'

'Don't worry, Dyl,' Nico said. 'You'll fit right in.'

'Freakin' shut up,' Dylan snapped. 'And don't call me Dyl. It's bad enough going to some hellhole brat camp, without you starting on me.'

Geri just pursed her lips. 'Discipline … discipline,' she tutted.

The large, white building was now identifiable as three separate houses. The biggest was in the centre – a low, sprawling concrete structure with small windows and a few thorny bushes by the front door. A man stood outside, arms folded.

5

'Camp Happiness isn't very nice-looking, is it?' Ketty said, disappointed.

'It's not supposed to be,' Geri snapped. 'You're here to learn to behave yourselves. It's perfectly adequate, with a good record on discipline.'

Nico muttered something from the back of the jeep.

'Most importantly, it's safe. No one here knows who you are so you'll be able to lie low while we make sure your identities are still secret from Damian Foster and Blake Carson and all the other criminals who'd give their eye teeth to get their hands on you.'

I gritted my teeth. The worst part of us being sent here was that, in the outside world, everyone apart from our parents thought we were dead. Geri had gone to extreme lengths over this. She'd exploded a bomb in our school, then changed all our records to say we'd died in the blast. She insisted this was necessary for our own protection but it made me angry – if Geri hadn't forced us to become the Medusa Project, we wouldn't *need* protecting.

Anyway, we were under strict instructions to keep our skills under wraps while we were at the camp. *That*, I didn't have a problem with. I hate being able to mind-read. It's an invasion of privacy. It's *wrong*.

The jeep juddered over rough paving stone and came to a halt. I opened my eyes. We'd arrived. The man who'd been standing by the door was now advancing towards us, a big smile on his face. He looked very Spanish – dark hair and eyes and the same olive skin as Nico. He pulled open Geri's door and extended a hand to help her out. The hot air surged into the car like somebody had trained a hairdryer on us.

'Welcome to Camp Felicidad. You must be Ms Paterson.'

I stared at him. Apart from a slight nasal twang in his voice, the man sounded English.

'Welcome.' The man glanced round at the four of us. I quickly averted my eyes, not wanting to make eye contact and be forced to dive into his mind.

'Do any of you young people speak Spanish?' the man said.

'Ed does,' Geri said, indicating me. 'And Dylan here's good at it too.'

Senor Fernandez looked at us expectantly.

'Hola,' Dylan said, sulkily.

'Como se llama usted?' I asked, trying to sound polite.

'You may call me Senor Fernandez,' the man replied. 'I hope your stay here will be fruitful. Now, I'm sure you're eager to get your bearings.' He stood back to make way for Geri and pointed towards the house. 'Beautiful ladies first.'

Geri smiled – one of those knowing smiles that basically mean the person knows they're being flattered but likes it anyway.

We followed them into the house. It was still steamily hot outside, despite the fact that the sun was so low in the sky. The contrast inside the house was startling. So cool I almost shivered. The thick stone walls clearly blocked out much of the heat. A fan blasted away in the corner. I blinked, taking in the stone flags on the floor, the reception desk in the corner and the long trestle table down the middle of the room.

'Looks like a hostel,' Ketty whispered in my ear. 'I thought it would be worse from what Dylan said about brat camps.'

'This is where we eat.' Senor Fernandez indicated the table with a sweep of his hand. 'Our other young people are busy with evening chores. You'll meet them a little later.' He turned to Geri. 'Is it to your satisfaction so far, Ms Paterson?'

Geri gave him a brisk nod. 'It seems suitably basic,' she said. 'Though to be honest, dear, I don't care what it looks like, so long as these kids learn some discipline while they're here.'

Ketty and Nico exchanged exasperated glances behind Geri's back.

'Of course.' Senor Fernandez gave a little bow. He led us down a corridor to the girls' quarters – a six-bed dorm, much bleaker than the one back at Fox Academy. The walls were plain white – no posters or pictures. Each bed was covered with a pale blue quilt and stood next to a small locker. The tops of the lockers were completely clear.

Geri nodded, approvingly.

'Clean and simple,' Fernandez said.

'. . . like a cell,' Nico muttered.

Senor Fernandez flashed a fierce look at him. 'Rule number one,' he snapped. 'Young people must ask for permission to speak.' His face relaxed. 'However, an adjustment period for new young people is only fair, so no demerits tonight.'

'De-what?' Nico said.

Senor Fernandez shook his head and made a clicking sound at the back of his throat. He turned his attention back

8

to Geri. 'The boys' room is identical, just in a different part of the building. Would you like to see that now?' he asked.

Geri hesitated, checking her watch. 'I really don't have time,' she said.

'Absolutely fine, of course, you need to get going.' Fernandez gestured back to the main lobby. 'Let me see you out.'

We left Dylan and Ketty in their room and followed Fernandez back down the corridor.

As we reached the lobby, Geri turned to me and Nico.

'Please use this as an opportunity to learn some discipline,' she said, with heavy emphasis. 'I'll call in to the camp phone one week from tonight to see how you're getting on.'

I nodded. Nico just stared sullenly at the floor.

'Right, well, goodbye then.' She took a step towards the front door.

'Let me see you to your car, Ms Paterson,' Fernandez said. He turned to Nico and me. 'You boys wait here. *Don't move.*'

Geri and Fernandez left. I sighed and looked round the room. The trestle table had been scrubbed so hard that the wood in the middle was almost white. The dresser behind was stacked with plates and glasses. There was no mess ... nothing that made it feel homely at all.

'Ed.'

I spun round. Nico was standing beside the door on the far side of the room, beyond the long table. He opened it softly and peered round. 'Come on,' he said quietly. 'There's a corridor down here, with a door and a window.'

'*Nico*, for goodness sake.' My heart thudded. 'That man told us to stay here.'

'Lighten up, man.' Nico made a face. 'I'm just gonna take a quick look. I'll be back before Senor Fussypants knows we were gone.' He disappeared through the door.

Muttering angrily to myself, I crossed the room towards him. It was all very well Nico saying he would was only taking a 'quick look'. If Fernandez came back and found him gone, I could just imagine how much trouble we would *both* be in.

I reached the door and peered round it. Nico was standing in a gloomy corridor, staring out of a window onto an empty, shaded courtyard.

'Come back,' I hissed.

Nico shook his head. 'We've got a second.' He frowned, still staring out at the courtyard. 'Where d'you think everyone is?' he whispered.

'Working, remember?' I said.

'Oh yeah. "The *young people* are doing their chores",' Nico said, in a fair imitation of Fernandez' voice. 'Don't you hate being called that ... young people? It's so patronising.'

'Nico, will you—'

'Jesus, man, *look*!' Nico held up his hand to silence me. '*Look*,' he repeated, pointing through the window. A line of five or six kids – some about our age, others younger – were crossing the bleak stone courtyard after a thickset man with a snake tattoo down one arm.

The kids were dressed shabbily, though they looked clean.

10

But there was something defeated about the way they were walking that sent a chill down my spine.

As we watched, one of the younger kids said something, and the man with the tattoo hit him across the head. The boy stumbled sideways, then carried on walking. My mouth fell open. I moved closer to the window.

Nico sucked in his breath. 'That doesn't look like the *young people* doing their chores, does it?'

I shook my head, frowning.

We watched for a moment longer. As they reached the edge of the toilets in the centre of the courtyard, Tattoo Man struck another member of the group, a skinny girl with long dark hair. The girl fell to the ground. The man pointed to her trailing shoe lace and the girl knelt, meekly, to tie it.

'Jesus Christ,' Nico breathed. 'What the hell *is* this place?'

I glanced back into the camp lobby. The front door was still firmly shut. I caught the echo of Geri's high tinkly laugh in the distance. She and Fernandez must still be talking.

I took a deep breath and joined Nico by the window. From here I could see the whole courtyard. It was paved with large stone slabs and flanked on one side by what looked like a barn and on the other by a white building similar in style to the main house. Apart from the toilets in the centre, the courtyard was empty.

As we watched, Tattoo Man and the other kids vanished round the side of the toilets, leaving the skinny dark-haired girl in plain view, still struggling with her shoelace.

Nico darted down the corridor to the door that led onto the

11

courtyard. He yanked on the handle. Locked. He raised his hand in the gesture he uses to perform telekinesis.

'What are you doing?' I said, appalled.

'Listen,' he said, urgently. 'If what we've just seen is typical of what goes on in this camp, then we need to find out and tell Geri before she leaves.' He twisted his hand. There was a click as the lock undid and the door sprang ajar. I stared, impressed in spite of myself. I'd never tell him this, but Nico's telekinetic skills are pretty amazing to watch.

Nico pushed the door open and stepped into the courtyard.

I hesitated for a second, then followed. Nico was right, we had to find out what we were letting ourselves in for.

The heat hit me hard. Even in the shade of the courtyard it was like stepping into an oven. I glanced round as we crept across the paving stones. No one at the windows. At least we wouldn't be spotted from inside the house.

Nico had already reached the girl. She jumped as he touched her shoulder. He said something in a low voice while I ran past and peered round the side of the hut.

The other kids and Tattoo Man were gathered next to a ramshackle old VW bus, parked in the shade of a single tree. Next to the bus was a huge wooden well, with a fenced area beyond. This area was strikingly lush and green compared to the arid desert all around us. Tattoo Man was talking in Spanish. His speech was too rapid for me to catch any of the words, but he was clearly barking out orders.

I turned back to Nico and the girl.

'Que?' she was whispering. 'Quien eres?'

Nico turned to me. 'I don't understand what she's saying,' he whispered.

I barely heard him. I was staring, transfixed, at the girl. I wasn't looking into her eyes – that would have meant automatically mindreading her – but I'd already seen they were beautiful: a sea-green colour that stood out against her tanned skin. And it wasn't just her eyes. *She* was beautiful. About my age, with a worried, oval face, a long nose and silky dark hair that curled onto her shoulders.

'*Ed*,' Nico hissed.

'She asked who we were,' I explained.

'Ed,' I said to the girl. 'Me llamo Ed. Este es Nico. Y tu? Como te llamas?'

The girl was trying to look into my eyes, but I kept my gaze averted.

'Luz,' she whispered. 'Me llamo Luz. You ... Eds, English ... please, help ...'

'What are you saying?' Nico hissed beside us.

'Just our names,' I said. 'She's called Luz.'

'Loos?' Nico said.

'Luz, donde estas?' Tattoo Man shouted from round the corner.

Luz froze. Nico grabbed my arm with one hand and Luz's with the other and dragged us into the WC marked *Senors* – the men's toilet.

We stood in the narrow, dimly lit corridor. A stench drifted out from the toilets.

'Ask her what the hell's going on here,' Nico demanded.

13

A second later, a shadow fell across the doorway. I held my breath and pressed my back against the cool concrete wall.

'LUZ, ven aqui!' It was the man, even angrier than before. He swore in Spanish, then said something I just about understood about there not being time for a toilet break.

He thought Luz was in the ladies' toilet next to this one.

Luz took a step towards the door. I grabbed her arm. I didn't dare speak in case the man heard us. If I wanted to know what was going on here, I was going to have to mind-read. I pulled Luz round until she met my eyes.

In a second I was inside her mind. People always freak when that happens the first time, and Luz was no exception. Her mind was jumping around, full of fear and confusion. Mind you, my own thoughts were jumping about just as badly.

Hola, I stammered – not knowing what else to thought-speak. *It's okay. Who is that man?*

Que? Luz's mind was still all over the place, her thought-speech tumbling out.

How this? A single strand of thought stood out above the rest: *We must quick ... Eds, English ... you just come in camp, no?*

Si. I tried to make my mind settle.

This place no es good. Senor Fernandez es bad man. You go. Tell persons ... help ...

Where are you going in the van?

Que?

Donde vas en el ... el coche grande?

Damn it, why did my Spanish have to desert me now?

14

No se ... I don't know ... Ed. Por favor. Ayudame.

Ayudame. Help me. My stomach turned over.

'*Luz!*' The man outside sounded very close. 'Are you in the *men's* toilet?' he said in Spanish.

Need go, Luz's thought-speech grew panicky. *Help.*

'Ed, leave it,' Nico hissed, right in my ear.

I will help, I promise. I broke the connection.

Luz burst through the door. We waited, holding our breath. I could hear the man yelling at her, then the slap of a hand, presumably making contact with Luz's head. I raged silently at the thought of her being hurt.

A few more seconds passed, then Nico peered out after her. 'They've gone, come on,' he said.

He slipped outside and raced across the courtyard.

I followed, more slowly, a large part of me wanting to find Luz. I could hear the bus revving up round the corner.

What was happening to her? Where was she being taken?

And then a large hand clamped down on my shoulder and Senor Fernandez's heavy, nasal voice sounded in my ear.

'Only in camp five minutes,' he said, 'and you, Ed, are already in the deepest of deep shits.'

15

2: PUNISHMENT

I was shaking as we walked inside. Fernadez took his hand off my shoulder only when we were back in the entrance area of the main building. Nico and the girls were standing round the long dining table at the back of the room. The girls were wide-eyed with shock. Nico's expression was a mix of guilt and concern. Clearly he'd managed to make it inside without being spotted by Fernandez or any of his workers.

'What were you doing outside?' Fernandez demanded.

'Where's G— er, Ms Paterson?' I said.

'Gone.' Fernandez glared at me. 'I'll ask you once more. What were you doing outside? *How* did you get outside?'

I thought rapidly. 'I needed to use the toilets in the courtyard,' I said. 'The door was open.'

I stared at the floor. The tiles were set in an alternating pattern of creams and browns. Across the room I could see Ketty fidgeting from side to side. I looked up at her, hoping she wasn't about to leap to my defence and get herself in trouble.

'You disobeyed a direct order from me. At Camp Felicidad, that's a punishable offence. Cause and effect. Simple.'

'Ed must have *really* needed to pee,' Ketty blurted out.

I blushed.

'You have to believe me,' she went on. 'Ed's the last person who'd go off on his own for no good reason.'

What was she saying? That I was easily led?

'Actually he wasn't on his own,' Nico chipped in. 'He was with me. We went outside together.'

Oh God. In spite of the mess I was in with Fernandez I couldn't help but feel annoyed with Nico. Couldn't he see that admitting he'd been with me hardly backed up my story about needing the loo?

Ketty flashed Nico an admiring glance. I supposed she was impressed by his loyalty. That made me feel even more annoyed.

'Silence,' Fernandez snapped. 'So, there were two of you, equally desperate to use the facilities? I don't think so. Now, tell me, what did you see?'

I took a deep breath. Maybe the best thing was just to explain what we'd seen ... ask Fernandez who the kids were. Nico was shaking his head at me. I avoided making eye contact with him. Aside from actually mind-reading the man – which would have given away the secret about our psychic abilities – putting Fernandez on the spot had to be the best way to get the truth.

'We saw some kids out the back, getting into a bus. I spoke to one of the girls. She said this, er ... it's not a good place, that the people here aren't treated well.'

17

Across the room, Nico groaned.

'Well, she's wrong,' Fernandez snapped. He hesitated, as if trying to decide something. Then he smiled. 'What you saw was a group of extremely violent young offenders. They were sent here by mistake. Somebody in the San Juan police department got their paperwork muddled up. They're supposed to be in a juvenile detention centre.'

'They didn't look violent ... and that doesn't excuse how they were being treated,' I stammered. 'I saw the man they were with – he hit one girl just for having her shoelace undone.'

Fernandez sighed. 'I am sure it seemed disproportionate to you, and I can assure you there is no corporal punishment here in camp. However, a slap or two is sometimes needed with these violent children. It may, in fact, prevent worse violence. Anyway, I am sure that the man who hit this girl was just frustrated at being sent all the way out here for nothing. It has nothing to do with the camp or me.'

I shook my head. I didn't believe Luz was a violent criminal. And if she had nothing to do with Fernandez, how did she know his name?

'But—'

'Enough. This discussion is over. Each of you boys will receive a demerit for your disobedience. Cindy will be here in a second to show you what to do.'

'What's a demerit?' Nico asked, but Fernandez was already halfway through the door.

My guts twisted into a knot. We stood in silence for a second. I could feel the others' eyes upon me.

18

'What the hell happened out there?' Dylan asked, accusingly.

Nico shrugged. 'No idea. The girl we saw only spoke Spanish – that's when she was actually speaking. Ed mind-read her for ages.'

'Did you, Ed?' Ketty sounded surprised.

I understood why. After all, I've gone on to Ketty more than anyone how much I hate my telepathy. Of course she'd be surprised at me using it. But with Luz I hadn't really thought about it.

The door slammed. I jumped. A small woman in a red tracksuit stood in the doorway. She had a thin face and narrow eyes – kind of mean-looking – with lips painted the same colour as her tracksuit. This must be Cindy.

'Demerit time …' the woman said, with an American accent. She pointed at me and Nico. 'You two. Twenty-five laps round the field. Now.'

A few minutes later we were out in the courtyard. The two buildings on either side of the main building were sprawling white squares. I hadn't really looked at them before. Now I noticed several boys looking out of the building on the right.

We walked round to where the bus had been earlier. The sun was low in the sky, the heat less intense. Beyond the complex the desert stretched away. Mountains stood, hazy, in the distance. Between us and the desert was the field. It was large and green, filled with rows of plants and earth beds.

Nico stared at Cindy in horror. 'You want us to run round that twenty-five times?'

'Make it fifty,' Cindy snapped. 'And if you stop for a second it'll be fifty more.'

'But it's still really hot,' Nico argued.

'You're just not used to it.' Cindy glanced at the setting sun.

'But still ... fifty laps?' I said.

'Go, before I make it a hundred.'

Nico grabbed my arm. We jogged off. I still couldn't take it in. Two days ago I'd had a life and a family and a school and a home.

Now I had nothing. Tears welled in my eyes. I suddenly ached to speak to my dad and stepmum. My chinos were already sticking to me and we hadn't even reached the field.

As we began our first lap, Nico muttered, 'Welcome to boot camp.'

The laps took me nearly two hours to complete. I stopped once, just for a moment, but Cindy appeared from nowhere and yelled at me to 'move your lazy ass', though she did bring us a couple of water bottles a bit later.

Nico's slightly longer stride meant we hardly ever ran side by side. I didn't mind. It was too tiring to talk while we were running anyway. At least someone was sharing this ordeal with me.

The boys I'd noticed before, at the window of one of the buildings, disappeared. I thought I saw Ketty once, glancing out of one of the main building windows, but it was hard to be sure.

The heat dropped off fast after about an hour, when the sun

finally set. The only light illuminating the field came from inside the three camp buildings. The desert beyond was pitch-black – the darkening sky showing only the tiniest of crescent moons among a million stars.

Towards the end of the run I lost count of my laps. Exhausted, I staggered round the field, somehow putting one foot in front of the other. It was all I could do not to cry. It had been a nightmareish few days – kidnapping, explosions, being told everyone thought we were dead ... On top of all that drama and danger, this was just too much for me.

Ahead of me, Nico stopped and left the field. He stood, clearly catching his breath, beside the well. Cindy appeared. She was talking as I ran past.

'That's fifty,' she called out. 'You can stop too, Ed.'

I nodded, too tired to speak, and flopped to the ground beside Nico. It was hard and dusty. I had blisters on my feet and my legs ached. I lay back and closed my eyes. I could have slept then and there, but Cindy kicked my leg.

'Up,' she ordered. 'You've missed supper, but Senor Fernandez says you can eat something in your room. Come with me.'

I got up and limped after her across the yard.

'Are you one of the teachers here?' I said.

'This is the last time I warn you, you have to ask permission to speak.'

I glanced at Nico. He rolled his eyes.

'Er ... permission to speak?' I stammered.

21

'Granted.'

I repeated my question.

'I'm Cindy Collins,' the woman said. 'I'm in charge of the Day Schedule.'

'Day Schedule?' I echoed.

'Up at 6 a.m. Chores until 8.30, then breakfast. Lessons. Lunch. Lessons. Chores. Supper. Chores. Lights out at 9 p.m.'

Nico let out a low whistle.

'That sounds ... er, hard work,' I said. Now I'd stopped running I realised just how sore my legs and feet were.

'It is,' Cindy snapped. 'So you might as well get used to it.'

She pointed at the door leading to the building on the left of the main house.

'In there. The bedroom's on your right. There's a bathroom on the left. Don't attempt to go in any of the storerooms or I'll slap you with a demerit before you can say "broken toe".'

'What is a demerit exactly?' I asked, but Cindy was already marching back to the main building.

Nico opened the door. 'At least that frigging run's over,' he said.

I followed him inside. Sounds were coming from the room on the right – the room I'd seen the boys looking out of.

'This is where she said the bedroom was.' I glanced at Nico.

'How bad can it be?' he asked.

He opened the door and we walked through. The room was as plain as the girls' accommodation we'd seen earlier, a far cry from the comfortable dorms at Fox Academy.

Six beds stood against the walls – three along each side –

with a small, bare locker beside each bed. Nothing on the plain white walls. A window, covered with a brown blind, was at the far end.

And three boys. They stood in a row in front of the window, arms folded.

None of them were smiling.

3: BOOT CAMP

I stared at the three boys. Two of them were virtually identical – about the same age as me and Nico, with short blondish hair and hard eyes. They both wore combats and T-shirts. Nothing fancy, but a lot smarter than what we'd seen the line of kids wearing earlier. The third boy was smaller – maybe nine or ten, with a reddish tinge to his wavy hair, pale blue eyes and round glasses. His skinny legs stuck out like twigs from his shorts.

'Hi.' Nico smiled. 'I'm Nico and this is Ed. Do any of you speak English?'

'I *am* English.' The smallest boy jutted his chin out. He sounded superior – his accent was very posh – but I sensed he was scared.

'Hi,' I said quickly. 'What's your name?'

'Tommy,' the boy said.

Silence. One of the blond boys prodded him. Tommy nodded.

'These two are Mateo and Miguel. Twins. I call them Mat and Mig.'

'Hola,' I said. 'Que tal?'

'Bien.' The slightly taller of the two boys had spoken. He had a pointier chin than his brother, and fuller lips. He launched into a rapid splurge of Spanish. I recognised only a few words.

'Mas despacio,' I interrupted. 'Slower.'

'Mig's asking what you did to be sent here,' Tommy explained. 'He's also saying that he and Mat are here 'cos they killed someone. But that's bollocks, it's me you want to watch out for.'

He glared at us from behind his glasses, but I could see his hands were shaking. Beside me, Nico snorted. I bit back my own smile.

'Thanks for the warning, Tommy,' I said.

'Hey, Tommy, why don't you tell Mat and Mig here that I murdered an entire roomful of people,' Nico said.

'No, Tommy, don't.' I shot Nico an irritated glance before launching into our cover stories. 'Tell them we're both here 'cause our parents sent us. We went to the same school but I dropped out because, let's face it, smoking weed is more fun. Nico stole his dad's credit card and used it to buy computer games that he sold to other people for a profit.'

I held my breath, hoping that Tommy would accept our stories without asking for more details. I didn't want to lie any more than was necessary.

Tommy nodded slowly. He turned to Mat and Mig and gabbled something I didn't understand.

Mat looked over at me. 'We no fight,' he said, firmly.

25

'No . . . I mean, yes,' I said. 'We no fight.'

Mat nodded. Relaxing, he turned to his brother and said something I couldn't hear. A moment later Mat and Mig wandered over to one of the beds. A jigsaw puzzle was laid out on the cover. They sat down beside it and started examining the pieces.

I turned back to Tommy. 'You speak Spanish well,' I said.

Tommy shrugged. 'My family live in Madrid.'

'Why are you here?' Nico asked.

Tommy shrugged again. 'Getting into fights, but only because I was picked on. It wasn't fair.'

'So what's it like here?' Nico said.

'Rubbish,' Tommy said. 'Chores all day. No TV. No internet.'

'*What?*' Nico said.

'Do they hit you?' I said, thinking of how I'd seen that man strike Luz.

'No,' Tommy acknowledged. 'It's just *really* strict. Most of the time we're working. This hour is the only free time we get. Fernandez is mean. He says everything's designed to break us down, make us fit for "parental consumption". That's how he puts it.'

I looked round the room again. It really was incredibly bare. The floor was completely empty, while the only sign of bed ownership was the creased edge of a photo peeking out from under the pillow of the bed nearest the window.

'That bed's mine,' Tommy said, following my gaze.

26

'That's fine,' I said. 'I'll take this one ... is that okay?' I pointed to the bed on the left, nearest the door. It was covered, like the others, with a plain navy sheet. A blanket was rolled up at the end of the bed.

Tommy nodded. 'Your stuff's over there.' He pointed behind the door. The small bags Nico and I had brought with us were propped against the wall. 'We didn't touch anything,' he added.

'How many people are in the camp?' Nico asked.

'This is all the boys.' Tommy made a face. 'There are a few girls too – mostly Spanish.'

I thought of Luz again.

'We met a Spanish girl earlier,' I said. 'Luz. I don't think she'd been here long. She was with some other kids, getting on a bus out the back. D'you know her ... them?'

'I *saw* them.' Tommy sat down on his bed. 'They arrived here in a police van earlier. That happens a lot. Kids arrive. They're kept separate from us, in the barn. Then after a while a bus or a car turns up to take them somewhere else.'

'Where do they go?' I asked, as Nico picked up our bags. He chucked mine on the bed I'd picked and took his to the bed opposite.

'Dunno.' Tommy lay back on his bed, hands under his head. 'Like I said, we're not allowed to speak to the police van kids.'

I frowned. Senor Fernandez had said Luz and the others were juvenile criminals, brought here by accident. But if their transition through Camp Felicidad was really a mistake, then why did it happen on a regular basis?

27

'Most people here come from rich families,' Tommy went on. 'Or at least families that can afford to send them. Average stay is about a month. I've been here six weeks.'

'Yeah?' I looked round. Mat and Mig were still sitting on one of the other beds now, completely absorbed in their jigsaw puzzle. 'What about them?'

'They've been here a fortnight so far,' Tommy explained. 'Sent down for persistent truanting.'

'I was about six the last time I did a jigsaw,' Nico muttered.

'Don't knock it,' I said. 'Doesn't sound like there's much else to do.'

Nico grunted. 'D'you think Ketty and Dylan are okay?'

'Who are they?' Tommy asked.

I quickly explained, giving the girls' cover stories. Ketty was supposedly in trouble for petty thieving; Dylan for constant disobedience.

'Let's go and find them.' Nico sat up.

I sat down on the edge of my bed. It was hard as rock, but at that moment I didn't care. The weariness from the long, punishing run I'd just done was creeping up my legs now. I wasn't at all sure I could have stood up again.

'I wouldn't,' Tommy said. 'If Cindy or Fernandez catch you – and they will – you'll get a demerit.'

'What *are* demerits?' Nico demanded.

'Black marks against your name,' Tommy explained. 'Everytime you do something wrong – break a rule ... answer back ... you get a demerit. That run they made you do earlier – that was because of a demerit, wasn't it?'

28

I nodded. 'So a demerit means a punishment?'

'Yup.' Tommy sighed. 'Five demerits in a week and you go into solitary. No one's allowed to speak to you for a whole day and you're not allowed to speak to them.'

The door opened. Cindy appeared with a tray covered with a cloth. She set it on the floor.

'Bread and cheese for Nico and Ed,' she said.

'Permission to speak.' Tommy sprang off his bed.

'Yes?' Cindy turned her mean little eyes on the boy.

'Instead of chores tomorrow morning, could I show Ed and Nico around?' he said. 'Explain how everything works?'

'No,' Cindy snapped. 'They'll learn fast enough without any special treatment.' She glanced from me to Nico. 'Lights out in forty-five minutes. Make the most of them. They'll be all the free time you get for twenty-four hours.' She left, shutting the door.

'Lights out at *nine*?' Nico sounded disgusted. 'I can't go to sleep that early, even after that frigging run.'

I let myself sink into the bed. I was starving hungry but it was suddenly too much effort to even make it from the bed to the tray. I closed my eyes. A few seconds later sleep took over – a hot, troubled sleep in which visions of Ketty and Luz swirled in my mind.

I woke, disorientated, to the sound of Spanish chatter. The sun was creeping brightly round the edges of the blind. Mat and Mig were already up and dressed. I got a change of clothes from my bag and went into the bathroom. It was basic. Just a sink, a toilet and a shower set into the wall behind a grubby shower curtain. I crossed the chipped white tiles and took a lukewarm shower, then dressed in fresh clothes.

Nico emerged, bleary-eyed, from the dorm as I left the bathroom.

'It's almost 6 a.m.' He yawned. 'Which means "chores", remember?'

I nodded. 'What d'you think we'll have to do?'

I found out a few minutes later, when Cindy arrived, with Ketty, Dylan and four other girls in tow. Outside, the sun was already beating down, baking the earth. I glanced at Ketty, catching her eye.

You okay? I thought-spoke, keeping my tone light.

I guess. Ketty's thought-speech felt anxious. *The other girls seem all right, though Dylan's managed to piss them off already. But that Cindy's a bitch and this place is unbelievable. You know we only get one hour of free time all day?*

I know.

I broke the connection as Cindy started explaining our early-morning chores.

'Tommy, take Nico and Ed to the barn and fetch spades and forks for everyone.' Cindy pointed to the field. 'Outdoor chores this morning are either digging soil for potatoes or working on the irrigation ditch. You three ...' she indicated Ketty, Mig and one of the other girls, 'you're on kitchen duty. Follow me.'

With a despairing look at Nico, Ketty followed Cindy indoors.

The barn was the building on the other side of the main

house from the one the boys' dorm was in. Large and ramshackle, it was a lot less well kept than the rest of the camp, with peeling paint on the walls and windows, and piles of machinery and equipment heaped haphazardly inside.

'Watch out for rats,' Tommy muttered, as we crossed the makeshift path towards a collection of tools leaning against the wall.

I glanced into the gloomy corners of the barn. A couple of bales of straw were stacked against the far wall beside a generator. We gathered an assortment of spades and digging forks and took them outside.

Mat led the way over to the field. 'You ... here,' Mat said, pointing from me and Nico to a large, dry earth bowl that I guessed must be the irrigation ditch Cindy had mentioned.

Dylan and Camila – a small Asian-looking girl with a round face – joined us as we started digging. Camila smiled shyly at us.

'Hi, there.' She spoke with a strong Spanish accent.

'Hi.' Nico and I smiled back.

We worked for a few moments. Camila started chatting to Nico. I could hear him giving her a basic outline of all of our cover stories.

I turned away and whispered to Dylan: 'How're you doing? How's Ketty?'

'I'm horrible,' she snapped back, leaning on her spade. 'This work sucks and the whole place is a total sty. My bed might as well be made of stone, the shower is lukewarm and I saw two cockroaches on the way out here.'

31

'Get on with it!' Cindy yelled from the main house.

Swearing, Dylan took up her spade again and dug. Nico had already shifted a fair bit of earth. I positioned myself next to him, trying to copy the way he put his weight behind the movement. Was he using a little telekinesis? I couldn't be sure.

The earth was dry and hard. Even making a dent in it was back-breaking. I looked round. Mat, Tommy and three of the girls were busy digging up rows of earth across the field. In our ditch, Camila was surprisingly effective with her spade, considering how tiny she was. Next to her, Dylan was working at half the speed. She kept up a steady flow of complaints.

'Jesus, this is ridiculous ... Oh, great, my ring's covered in mud and I've broken *two* freakin' nails now ... this patch of earth is as hard as that Cindy's ass ...'

We worked for nearly two hours, stopping only once when Cindy brought out bottles of water for us.

Still stiff from yesterday, by the time we stopped I was completely exhausted again – and starving. We trooped inside for breakfast, down a series of corridors I hadn't see before. Doors led off on either side. As we passed, I caught glimpses of a large kitchen, and Senor Fernandez in another room that looked like an office. He was on the phone and didn't look up as we passed.

I devoured my breakfast of bacon and rolls. It was surprisingly good, though I was so hungry I'd have eaten anything. I glugged down two glasses of milk, then looked round for

Ketty. She was at the other end of the table, next to Nico. They were deep in conversation, their heads close together.

I felt a familiar stab of jealousy, but tried to shake it off. Boot camp was going to be hard enough, without letting myself get annoyed about Nico and Ketty. I chatted a little to Camila and Tommy. It was obvious straight away that little Tommy was developing a bit of a thing for Ketty, while Camila kept throwing longing glances in Nico's direction.

I sighed. Why did no one ever have a crush on me?

After breakfast we were taken to another new room and sat around a large table. Maths and history papers were brought in by a young black guy called Don who I hadn't seen before. Don sat at the front of the room and explained in a heavy Spanish accent that we were to work through the maths – there were Spanish copies for Mat, Mig and the Spanish girls; English for the rest of us – then copy the history information into workbooks.

I looked at the papers. The maths was stuff I'd done over a year ago. Easy. The history was all about Africa and the way the different countries had achieved independence in the last century. Reading it was quite interesting. Copying it out was really dull.

I worked steadily for about half an hour, then looked up. Tommy was still struggling on the first page of the maths paper. Poor kid. What were they doing giving him the same work as the rest of us? He was at least three years younger than anyone else here. The Spanish kids were all bent over their papers, though I could see Mig and one of the girls passing each other notes when Don wasn't looking.

Ketty and Dylan both appeared to be working too. So was Nico. No, wait, he wasn't really looking at the history information at all. He was staring into space, gently nodding his head. I peered under the table. A trailing wire led from a tiny MP3 player on his lap, into his shirt.

I prodded his arm and caught his eye.

What are you doing?

Camila lent me her player. Dunno how she managed to hang on to it, but some of it's cool.

How typical was that? I rolled my eyes and broke the connection before Dom noticed us staring at each other. He'd already given Dylan a demerit for complaining about having to do maths.

Eventually the session ended. As we left the room I caught up with Ketty.

'Have you ever done anything more boring in your life?' I said.

'I know,' she whispered.

We headed to the kitchen where Cindy organised us into a sandwich-making line. We ate outside in the shade. Except for Dylan, whose demerit punishment, it turned out, was to spend her lunch break sorting out some of the junk in the barn.

It was blisteringly hot – with virtually no breeze. My shirt was soaked with sweat in minutes. I only had one T-shirt left.

'Permission to speak,' I said.

'Granted,' Cindy barked.

'How do we clean our clothes?' I asked.

Behind me, Nico sniggered. 'Go, Chino Boy,' he whispered too quietly for Cindy to hear.

'You and Camila are on laundry duty this afternoon,' she said. 'You'll see how it works then.'

After lunch we did two more hours of ultra-boring lessons, then went on to afternoon chores. This time Dylan and Nico were both included in kitchen duty, while Ketty was sent to the barn to sand and paint some old chairs with Mig, Mat and Tommy.

'It's one of the things the camp does,' Tommy explained. 'Fixing up furniture then selling it on to junk shops.'

I trudged off to the laundry area – next to the kitchen – with Camila, who kept asking annoying questions about Nico such as where he was from and what kind of music he liked and if he had a girlfriend. I told her I hardly knew him and worked on in silence.

Water was heavily rationed, so we were limited to one bowl of soapy lukewarm water for washing everyone's clothes and one bowl for rinsing.

It was yet more tiring work. I was relieved to finish and eat dinner – a meat stew with potatoes. After dinner there were more chores. This time I was in the kitchen, washing up all the plates and bowls and pans from the meal. By the time I'd finished, my hands were red and raw from the water – and my whole body ached.

We were in our dorms at 8 p.m. and Senor Fernandez

came to switch off the light at 9 p.m. I could hear the others whispering as I fell into another troubled half-sleep – where images of Luz mingled with worries about Mum and Dad. Sandra's really my stepmum, but I call her Mum. Dad married her after my real mum died when I was four and my sister, Amy, was just a year old. Dad and Sandra went on and had another girl, Kim, so I guess we're quite a big family now.

Anyway, camp had been so busy during the day I hadn't had time to think about any of my family, but as I drifted off to sleep, I wondered how they were and whether they were thinking about me. If only I could have spoken to them, but the only phone was in Senor Fernandez' office and we were forbidden from using it. For the first time I wondered if it might be possible to mind-read at a distance – real telepathy – but I had no idea how to even start to do that.

The next day passed in a similar way. And the one after that – a constant sucession of physically demanding labour and mentally unstimulating schoolwork where thoughts of Luz crept, regularly, into my mind. Like Ketty, I did my best to stay out of trouble.

It wasn't hard. As Tommy had said, the camp was very strict but, once you knew the rules, it was easy enough to follow them. Nico, of course, pushed things – he even sneaked out after lights out to visit Ketty on the second night, though he came back within five minutes, declaring Fernandez was on the prowl. Dylan seemed to have annoyed everyone. Cindy particularly seemed to hate her, giving her demerits at the drop of a hat.

Apart from at mealtimes – when he sat apart from the rest of us – and when he came to switch lights out at the end of the day, we hardly ever saw Senor Fernandez. And then, at the end of the third day, Nico came up to me just before lights out. The dorm was fairly quiet. Mat and Mig were doing another jigsaw. A piece was missing and both of them were convinced Tommy had taken it. Tommy, meanwhile, was arguing, loudly, that he hadn't.

'We can't stay here, man,' Nico muttered. 'This dorm's like a frigging youth club and Fergus would go ballistic if he knew what Fernandez was making us do – all that hard labour in the field.'

It was always strange hearing Nico talk about Mr Fox in such a familiar way. Sometimes I forgot Fergus Fox was his stepfather, as well as our head teacher. I wondered if Nico missed him as much as I missed my dad and stepmum.

I sighed. 'Mr Fox doesn't have a choice about us being here. Geri's the only one who can get us out and I don't think she's going to be all that bothered about us having to dig ditches – she'll think it's good discipline. I mean, Fernandez is hardly in the same league as ...' I paused, remembering the names of the bad guys we'd been up against, '... as, say, Blake Carson ...'

'I know, but —' Nico started

'Anyway, what can we do? There's desert everywhere you look. We wouldn't last five minutes if we ran away – and even if we could drive, we don't know where the keys to Fernandez's car are.'

'There's a phone in his office,' Nico whispered. 'I'm going

to sneak into the main building and use it tonight. Call Geri on that emergency number she gave us.'

I stared at him. 'But she'll phone here at the end of the week anyway.'

'I'm not waiting for her to call and then have Fernandez listening in to the conversation, ready to tell her we're exaggerating everything. Jesus,' Nico hissed. 'I'll tell her we're being beaten up by the staff on a daily basis if it'll get us out of here. I need you to keep lookout. Will you help?'

'But . . .' I stared at him. 'What if we're caught?'

'Then we'll get ten frigging demerits.' Nico sighed. 'It's worth a try, isn't it?'

I stared at him. Fernandez's office didn't just contain a phone. There must be files and papers in there. Maybe one of them would explain where Luz had been taken. Meeting her felt like a dream, now, but I hadn't forgotten my promise to help her. If I could tell Geri where she was, Medusa HQ could at least check she was okay.

'Okay,' I said to him. 'Yes, let's do it.'

4: ESCONDITE

Nico and I went to bed – and to sleep – at the same time as the others. We were both knackered from three full-on days of hard work and knew we'd have to wait until the middle of the night before attempting to break into the main building and use the phone in Fernandez' office.

As our mobiles had been taken away before we left Fox Academy, the only way we had of setting an alarm was my watch. I left it on my pillow, timed to go off at 2 a.m. I was deeply asleep when it beeped beside me, so it took me a couple of seconds to stop the thing. I sat up, looking round in the pitch dark.

'What was that?' Tommy croaked sleepily from his bed.

'Just my watch going off,' I whispered. 'Sorry, go back to sleep.'

Tommy snuffled into his pillow as Nico crept over.

'Give it ten minutes,' he whispered, 'make sure the others are properly asleep.'

We waited in silence. All I could hear was my own breathing.

After what felt like ages, I tiptoed over to Tommy's bed. He was lying on his front, curled up like a baby, sucking his thumb. I watched the outline of his chest rise and fall evenly a couple of times. Well, that settled it. He was definitely asleep. There was no way he'd be faking with his thumb in his mouth.

Nico was standing between Mat and Mig's beds.

'They're well out of it,' he whispered.

'Come on, then. Let's go.'

The door that led outside was locked. Nico raised his hand and made a twisting motion. Telekinesis. With a soft click the lock sprang back. We padded across the courtyard. In the depths of night it was surprisingly cool. A bright moon hung clear in the sky, casting a gentle light across the three buildings.

The two bolts on the inside of the door into the main building scraped against the wall as Nico drew them back telekinetically. I held my breath, hoping no one inside would hear. We had no idea where Fernandez, Cindy or Don slept, though I was guessing their rooms were near the girls' dorm.

'Hurry up,' I whispered.

Nico waved his hand across the lock on the door. Another click. The door sprang open. We were inside.

'So far, so easy,' Nico murmured.

'Don't get cocky,' I whispered as we reached Fernandez's office door.

Nico rolled his eyes. 'Man, you sound just like Ketty.'

The office door was locked too. Nico focused for a second.

40

This time the lock turned silently. Nico pushed at the door and it swung open.

I followed him into the office. I'd only seen it through the open door before. It was larger than I'd realised. A row of filing cabinets stood down one side of the room. A desk cluttered with a PC, several books and a mountain of papers stood under the window, bathed in moonlight. Nico flicked the wall switch but no light came on.

'The generator's probably turned off overnight,' I muttered.

He nodded. 'At least there's moonlight.' He headed for the phone which was perched at one end of the desk.

I went over to the filing cabinets. How on earth was I going to find out anything about Luz among all the information in here?

I took out my little torch and scanned the drawers fast. They were labelled with numbers. I pulled a few open at random. Bills, brochures, repair estimates. I flicked through the papers as quickly as possible.

Across the room, Nico was dialling a number.

I checked another file. A bunch of invoices. Nothing that looked remotely connected to the kids staying at the camp.

'Ed, come here,' Nico whispered. 'This isn't working.'

'What did you dial? I asked.

'Geri's emergency number,' Nico said. 'I'm just getting an engaged signal.'

'Were you using the right international code?' I said.

'What?' Nico stared at me. 'How the frigging hell do I

41

work out what *that* is? Geri said we could use this number to reach her from *anywhere*.'

This was true. I remembered her handing out the number when she briefed us before our first mission. 'Well maybe you misdialled. Try it again.'

I turned back to the filing cabinets. The next drawer I tried was locked. I stared at it for a second before remembering who I was with.

'Nico?' I said.

'What?' He looked up from the number pad on the front of the phone.

'Could you open these drawers for me?'

Nico rolled his eyes. '*Why?*'

'Please.'

He peered at the drawer for a few seconds. With a twist of his hand, the locks sprang back.

Nico turned back to the phone. I pulled the drawer open. Sheaves of papers. I pulled out a bunch and rifled through them. Nothing that made any sense to me. And there were four more cabinets, all full of drawers just like this one. The information about Luz and the other police van kids – if it was here at all – could be in any one of them.

My guts twisted. How long had we been in here? Nico was still hanging on the phone, frowning.

'Maybe what you think is an engaged tone is actually some weird international ringtone,' I suggested. 'Stay on the line.'

Nico nodded. I shut the drawer, scanning the front of the

42

cabinets, trying to make sense of the numbers on the drawer fronts. They didn't follow on in any kind of order: 20 … 05, 20 … 08, 20 … 06 .

Of course. My heart leaped. The numbers were dates … years … All I had to do was find this year and the information about Luz was *bound* to be inside.

I scurried along the line. Nico was sitting on Fernandez's desk now, peering out of the window, the phone in his hand.

My heart was beating fast as I pulled open this year's drawer. There were fewer folders than in the other drawers. Not surprising, considering we were only in April. I yanked out a sheaf of papers and scanned them quickly.

Loads of kids I didn't know. Then a sheet on Tommy, then Camila. Then Mat and Mig and the Spanish girls. I sped up, not looking at them properly. Soon I found one with my name on it, containing all the details of my cover story. Similar papers for Nico, Ketty and Dylan were underneath.

There was nothing on Luz.

I reached inside the drawer, clawing into the back of it. My hand made contact with something soft. Surely not the back of the filing cabinet. I felt round the edges. A padded bag, taped to the back wall of the drawer. I yanked it out. The tape made a ripping noise as it pulled easily away from the drawer. I got the impression it had been attached and removed several times.

'What the hell are you doing?' Nico hissed.

But I barely heard him. I stared at the outside of the bag – it

43

was a plain, yellow padded envelope with just one word – *Escondite* – written on the outside in thick black ink. I shoved my hand inside and yanked out a bundle of papers. The word *policia* – 'police' – hit me straight off – it was written at the top of the first sheet and on the next few. I flicked through them. These were some kind of official forms – all written in Spanish. Most of them had kids' photographs pinned to the top. My heart thudded. From the Spanish I knew, I was sure these were police reports on children in trouble with the law. Could these be the police van kids? The ones Tommy said came and went from the camp? Why would Fernandez have all their details on file?

Sweat trickled down my neck as I scanned through the photos pinned to the sheets, searching for Luz.

Across the room, Nico had hung up and was dialling again, swearing under his breath.

A boy, two more, then a girl ... *There*. Luz's face stared back at me from her picture. Despite the fuzzy lines of the photo she looked beautiful – her sea-green eyes huge in her face. I unclipped the photo and held my torch closer.

'*Ed!*' Nico gasped. 'Listen!'

I turned towards the door, shoving the torch and picture of Luz into my pocket. The unmistakable sound of footsteps thumped down the corridor outside.

Nico and I stared at each other for a split second.

'Hide!' he whispered, putting down the phone. He ducked behind the desk.

I shoved the police reports back in the padded envelope,

44

pressed the envelope and tape back into place and pushed the drawer shut.

As I squeezed into the space between the end filing cabinet and the wall, Nico raised his hand slightly and twisted it. All the drawers clicked gently shut.

And then the door opened and Fernandez walked in.

5: DEMERITS

I held my breath as Fernandez marched straight to the desk where Nico was hiding.

'You little bastard,' he snapped, hauling Nico up from behind the desk by his hair.

'Ow,' Nico yelped.

I froze, shrinking into the shadows ... praying he wouldn't see me.

'What the hell are you doing in here, Nico?' Fernandez glanced round at the desk, his gaze sweeping from the PC to the books to the papers. His eyes lit on the phone. 'You were trying to *call* someone, weren't you?'

Fernandez swore. He was standing sideways on to me. If he'd looked round he'd have seen me. But he didn't look round. His full attention was on Nico. He moved closer, fury filling his face. His hands gripped Nico's neck.

My heart pounded. Why wasn't Nico using telekinesis to stop him?

A strangled squeak escaped from Nico's throat. His eyes

were bulging, his face turning purple. Fernandez was trying to kill him. I stood up. Lunged towards the desk.

'Stop!' I said.

Fernandez spun round, letting go of Nico, who fell, gasping, against the desk.

'*You?*' He loomed over me. He grabbed my arm and swore, his breath fierce and hot against my forehead.

Nico was still bent over the desk, clutching his throat.

I stood, panting, terrified. Fernandez shook my arm, jerking my head up. Before I could think or move, our eyes met. With a whoosh I was inside his head.

Fury. Blazing rage at the front of his mind. Then shock at my presence.

I shut my eyes, breaking the connection. It had only lasted a fraction of a second.

Surely that wasn't enough time for Fernandez to understand what had happened?

To know that I'd been inside his mind.

He stood, breathing heavily, staring at me.

I raced over to Nico, pulled him upright and dragged him back to the door.

'What was that?' Fernandez gasped.

'We didn't get through on the phone,' I said, ignoring the question. 'We didn't speak to anyone.'

'Of course you didn't, the phone is locked.' Fernandez stared at me like I was some kind of alien.

'So we'll go back to bed, then.' I edged closer to the door.

'How did you get into the building . . . the office?'

47

'Someone left the doors unlocked,' I lied, still heading for the door.

'Stop.' Fernandez frowned. 'Wait.'

I stood still, letting go of Nico's arm. I fixed my gaze on the tiled office floor at my feet.

'What did you just do ...?' Fernandez said. 'Just now, when I looked at you, it felt for a second like you were ... were inside my *head* ...'

'I don't know what you mean,' I said.

Beside me, Nico coughed.

Fernandez's face hardened. 'Look at me again.'

No. I carried on staring at the floor.

'Ed!' Fernandez grabbed my chin and forced my head up. 'Look at me!'

I shut my eyes. Fernandez dug his fingers into my face till it *really* hurt.

'Do it, or I'll break your jaw,' he hissed.

Praying that, against all the odds, I'd be able to avoid mind-reading him, I turned my eyes reluctantly upwards. *Don't jump into his mind. Don't jump—*

Whoosh. I was inside his head again. No way of stopping it. *Damn.* This time I sensed curiosity. And fear. For a second I managed to keep my own thoughts still, and then I remembered the envelope I'd found in the filing cabinet drawer. Before I could stop myself I was diving in, probing his thoughts.

What happened to the girl from the first day? Where are the police van kids?

Immediately I felt his mind throw up the information.

48

A place name he was instinctively trying to hide – it was coming . . . coming . . .

Ed?

Fernandez's thought-speech hit me like a splash of cold water. What the hell was I doing, giving myself away like this? I shut my eyes and broke the connection.

What an idiot.

Freed from the telepathy, Fernandez' questions spilled out loud. 'How did you read my thoughts? How did you ask me that question without speaking?'

'It was nothing,' I said. 'Just a trick.'

Fernandez frowned. He didn't look convinced. 'Why were you asking about those kids? I already told you. They were juvenile criminals. They'll be inside a detention centre by now.'

'I just wondered if . . . er, if they were okay,' I said quickly. I felt for the small photo of Luz in my pocket.

Beside me, Nico stiffened. I held my breath, praying Fernandez would believe me. He shook his head.

'Two demerits each,' he said. 'I'll sort out the punishments tomorrow.'

He marched us back to the dorm and double-locked the outer door.

The other three were still sleeping – Mat and Mig emitting gentle snores and Tommy sucking his thumb. Nico stumbled to his bed and lay down.

I went over. It was a clear night and the moon was shining directly in through the window, casting a silver beam of light across Nico's face.

'Are you okay?' I whispered.

'Yes,' Nico said. 'He wasn't really going to hurt me. Just scare me.'

'Why didn't you stop him with telekinesis?'

'For the same reason you tried to lie about getting inside his mind.' Nico sighed. 'Have you forgotten how Carson and all the other frigging bad guys we've had to deal with tried to use our abilities to get what they wanted? You know how I feel about Geri, but she was right about that: Our number one priority is to keep what we can do a secret.'

I stared at him.

'How come you mind-read Fernandez, anyway?' he said. 'Why didn't you stop yourself?'

'He'd already seen what I could do that first time by accident,' I stammered. 'Then, the second time, when he made me look at him, I couldn't help it. You *know* that if I make eye contact I can't hold back.'

'Yeah, I know,' Nico muttered disparagingly. He sat up. 'At least tell me you saw something useful. Something that might help us get out of here ...'

'I didn't see *anything* in Fernandez's mind. I was deliberately trying *not* to mind-read him.' I could feel my face reddening. It wasn't fair of Nico to have a go at me about this. 'But, before, I did find an envelope of police reports in the filing cabinet. It had a strange word written on it – *Escondite*. I'm not sure what it means, though.'

Nico lay back on his bed with a frustrated sigh. 'So you're

telling me you've just given away the fact that you can mind-read – for nothing.'

There was a long pause. 'I *told* you, I couldn't stop.' I could hear how defensive I sounded. 'It doesn't matter. Fernandez thinks it was just some trick.'

'Let's hope so.' Nico rubbed his eyes. 'Why were you looking for police reports in those filing cabinets anyway?'

I fingered the photo of Luz in my pocket again.

'Information – on us, the police van kids that come through here . . . the ones we saw . . . that Tommy told us about. I don't think Fernandez is officially supposed to have anything to do with them.'

'For God's sake, Ed, man.' Nico groaned. 'Never mind all of that. How are we going to get out of here now?'

There was an atmosphere in the camp the next morning. I could feel it as soon as Cindy called us for morning chores. She was in an evil mood, barking at everyone to hurry and giving Mig a demerit just for dropping his spade. I guessed that Fernandez must have bawled her out for believing she'd left the doors unlocked last night.

Ketty was almost in tears when she heard about Fernandez finding Nico and me in his office. Even Dylan looked shaken. She had picked up a fifth demerit late last night for talking back to Cindy at lights out and was now officially 'in solitary', which meant, as Cindy explained, that after breakfast she would be put to work in the barn on her own for the entire day. Anyone caught attempting to speak to

51

her, Cindy warned, would themselves be given a demerit.

We didn't see Fernandez until breakfast. He stood at the head of the dining table as we filed in, radiating fury. Everyone fell silent.

'Discipline,' Fernandez said, drawing himself up to his full height, 'is the be-all and end-all of Camp Felicidad. Without that we have nothing.' He paused. 'And in the past three days discipline has been in short supply.' He turned to Dylan. 'Five demerits in two days is a sign of weakness and a lack of self-respect.'

Dylan shrugged. Fernandez cleared his throat. 'Nico and Ed each earned two demerits last night for being out of their dorm after lights out. Nico's punishment is to spend the rest of the day digging the new well.'

There was a gasp from Tommy. I glanced at him and he whispered, 'That well is hard labour. They've been working on it for months and it makes digging potato patches in the field look like eating cake.'

I looked back at Fernandez. What the hell did he have in store for me?

He turned his dark eyes on me. I looked away, my face burning.

'Ed will take his demerits by working all his shifts today in the kitchen.'

I looked up. A low – and disgruntled – murmur swept round the room. Kitchen duty was widely accepted as the easiest chore option. No way was it normally used as a demerit punishment.

'Silence,' Fernandez snapped. He strode out of the room.

I sat, looking down at my lap, feeling everyone else's gaze upon me. Tommy, who was sitting next to me, leaned across and whispered, 'How come he's letting you off so light?'

I shook my head. I had no idea – maybe kitchen chores would involve something disgusting today, worse than the fish gutting I'd done the evening before last.

As breakfast finished, everyone filed out. Ketty was on breakfast duty with me.

'What were you and Nico *thinking* last night?' she asked as we cleared the plates and bowls onto trays. 'Surely you realised Fernandez would have disabled his office phone when he wasn't there?'

I shook my head, then explained how I'd been trying to work out what Fernandez was doing with the police van kids – and what information he held on us. I mentioned Luz too, though not how much I'd wanted to find out about her.

'Please be careful, Ed,' Ketty said, looking up at me with anxious, golden-brown eyes. 'I want to get out of here us much as you do, but we can't mess with Fernandez ... I keep trying to see into the future and I can't. I don't know why.' She shuddered. 'I just know that I'd hate it if you got hurt.'

I stared at a spot to the left of her eyes, feeling my face going red again.

'There's something else,' I stammered. 'Fernandez knows I can mind-read.'

'What?' Ketty said, her eyes widening. 'How?'

I explained what had happened while Ketty ran a bowl of

washing-up water, her forehead screwed up into a frown. She was silent for a while.

'Maybe that's why Fernandez hasn't punished you properly yet for breaking into his office last night,' she said at last, 'because he's realised you can mind-read and wants more time to work out what to do about it.'

I shrugged, following Ketty's gaze out of the kitchen window. The new well was clearly some way in the distance, beyond the field. I could just make out the top of Nico's head, deep inside it. Every few seconds a shovelful of earth appeared, tossed out of the hole he was digging.

'Is he using telekinesis to do that?'

'Course he is – and he's getting really good at it too,' Ketty said. She glanced sideways at me and smiled proudly. 'You know what he's like.'

'Yeah,' I said. 'I know.'

The rest of the day passed easily enough. Spurred on by my discovery of the *Escondite* files, I made my first serious attempt to contact Mum and Dad by remote telepathy, willing my brain to find theirs, wherever they were.

All I got was a headache.

I did at least find out what *Escondite* meant, though – *hiding place*.

Fernandez didn't reappear for the rest of the day. Cindy remained in a foul mood, snapping at me three times for peeling potatoes badly, leaving smear marks on the washing-up and spilling a pint of milk on the kitchen floor. At one point

54

she marched me across to the barn to fetch a fresh mop. Dylan was in there alone, gluing a chair leg together. I glanced at her as I fetched the mop, but she didn't look round.

Nico joined us for supper, though Dylan was made to eat alone in the barn. He was in quite a good mood, considering he'd been outside in the heat all day. He sat next to Ketty, telling her in a low whisper how he'd perfected the telekinetic act of digging earth with his spade without actually touching it.

'Ed.' Fernandez's voice appeared from nowhere.

I turned as he walked over.

'Come on.' He indicated the door.

'What ... er, where ...?'

'I didn't give you permission to speak,' Fernandez snapped. 'Follow me.'

I cast a swift look round at Ketty and Nico. They stared up at us, open-mouthed.

I wanted to mind-read with Ketty, but I didn't dare do it right under Fernandez's nose. So I turned and followed him out of the room.

He led me outside to the front of the main building. I hadn't been out here since our first day. This time I took in details I hadn't before, like the rubber tyre propped up against the wall and the faded yellow ribbon someone had tied in one of the thorny bushes by the front door.

Fernandez strode over to his car – a battered old Ford. 'Get in.'

As I opened the door my heart started thumping. God

55

knows I hated Camp Felicidad, but no way did I want to be leaving like this – without the others and not knowing where I was going.

We set off, into the desert. The mountain range was behind us, the sun low in the sky to our rights. Around us, sand stretched out in all directions. Bleak and bare.

Fernandez eyed me curiously. 'Tell me how far this telepathy thing of yours goes,' he said.

'It isn't telepathy,' I lied. 'I told you, it's just a trick.'

Fernandez snorted. 'No way,' he said. 'I could feel you last night – your voice inside my head, reading my thoughts and telling me your own.'

I looked down. Oh God. Nico was right. I really had given myself away – and for no advantage whatsoever.

'So ...' Fernandez went on. 'Can you tell what I'm thinking all the time? Or just when you look at me?'

There was no point in pretending any more.

'Only when I look at you,' I said. There was a pause. I took a deep breath. 'Why?'

Fernandez changed gear to negotiate a particularly rocky stretch of road.

'You'll see in two hours,' he said, a nasty smile creeping across his face. 'You'll see.'

6: THE SHOW

What on earth was Fernandez planning? I sat back, feeling anxious, as shadows spread across the desert and Camp Felicidad became a tiny white dot in the rear-view mirror.

Half an hour passed. The heat of the day eased and the sun sank quickly in the sky. So far we hadn't passed a single car or building. And then Fernandez rounded a bend and a petrol station came into view. He pulled up at one of the pumps. A boy came running out.

'Hola, senor.'

'Hola.' Fernandez jumped down from the jeep, a long stream of Spanish that I couldn't follow issuing from his mouth.

I sat back as the boy darted over to the petrol pump and unwound the hose. Fernandez locked me in and disappeared inside the corrugated-iron-roofed hut across the forecourt. A breeze through the tiny slit he'd left open in the window of the jeep felt cool against my hot face. I turned. The boy was busy filling up the car. I half-thought of banging on the window to attract his attention … pleading with him to help me escape … but before the thought had fully formed in my mind, Fernandez was back.

He strode towards the jeep, unlocking it as he marched. He paused to thank the boy, pressing a few coins into his palm, then jumped into the jeep and pulled away.

I wanted to ask again where we were going, but there seemed little point.

'Permission to speak?' I said.

'Granted,' Fernandez replied, as we headed into the desert again.

'How come your English is so good?' I asked.

Fernandez glanced at me. 'I went to an International School in the south of Spain for five years,' he said. 'I speak Spanish, English and French equally well.'

I waited in case he was going to say more, but he didn't. The petrol station was now well behind us. I closed my eyes and thought about Mum and Dad again. Dad had always been hard on me – pushing me to toughen up. He'd probably think being in camp was good for me. But my stepmum would definitely be worrying. I wondered if she was okay. And what about my sisters? Did they even know I was still alive? Or had Mum and Dad told them I'd been killed in the explosion at Fox Academy?

If only I could make contact with them.

I tried to focus on their faces, imagining the whole family. Mum in the kitchen, busy with dinner. Dad getting in from work complaining about his latest contract – an incomplete delivery, a rude client, an unreliable labourer. And Amy and Kim sitting round the kitchen table eating biscuits and doing their homework.

I visualised each one in turn, imagining I was staring into their eyes. Nothing happened. I felt overwhelmed with despair. My failed attempts at remote telepathy were just making my homesickness worse. I opened my eyes and focused on the view outside the window, determined to stop thinking about my family for the moment.

In the distance, a skyline of buildings gradually emerged. A cluster of white houses. A town. Was this where we were going?

Fernandez drove into the empty streets, and past a row of shops. It was properly dusk now and lights were on inside several of the houses we passed. My heartbeat fastened. This was a chance to get away ... all I had to do was give Fernandez the slip – find an adult who'd understand my Spanish. In my head, I rehearsed what I would say: *Ayudame, por favor. El hombre es malo. Quiero usar el telefono.*

It wasn't good Spanish, but it would get my point across.

Fernandez stopped outside a low, brick building surrounded by fairy lights. A sign hung from the door: *Casa Madelina.*

'We're in San Juan,' he said, matter-of-factly. 'This is the main bar.'

'Why are we here?' I asked.

Fernandez grinned. 'For tonight's show,' he said. 'A testing ground for fresh talent.'

'What fresh talent?' I said.

The grin deepened. 'Yours.'

'What?' I stared at him. 'What d'you mean?'

Fernandez switched off the car engine and took out the key. His face was suddenly serious. 'The Madelina is a local bar with an open mic policy. At a certain point every evening Jorge, the owner, lets a couple of punters get up on stage and do their thing. It's mostly locals who fancy themselves as singer/songwriters, though sometimes you get so-called comedians and I once saw a juggler here. There's never anyone good. People come for a laugh and a few beers.' Fernandez paused. 'You're going to take their breath away with that mind-reading thing you do.'

'What?' My heart raced. 'It isn't mind-reading,' I said quickly. 'I told you, it's just a trick.'

'Whatever it is, it works,' Fernandez said. 'You *knew* what I was thinking last night. I could feel you inside my head.'

A million anxieties crowded my mind. He was expecting me to use my telepathy when my biggest priority was to keep my Gift secret. Not to mention having to stand up in front of an audience of adult Spaniards and 'perform'.

'But I can't,' I pleaded, thinking fast. 'They'll all be thinking in Spanish ...'

'Then think back in Spanish.' Fernandez opened the locks on the car doors. 'You've got enough basic language to do that – I've heard you. I'll introduce you to the audience. All you have to do is tell them what they're thinking. Just remember that if you don't ...' he paused, 'you and your friends will *drown* under demerits.'

60

He leaped out of the car and was round to my side in seconds. He held the door open as I stepped out. My head spun. What the hell was I supposed to do now? I stumbled inside, Fernandez at my side.

Casa Madelina was dark and smoky. It took a few seconds for my eyes to adjust to the gloomy, candlelit interior. The bar wasn't large – just a few round tables with a bar serving drinks down one side and a small stage area at the end. Most of the tables were occupied by dark-haired, middle-aged men, at least half of whom were smoking. I could only see one woman – also middle-aged – in a low-cut pink top. She glanced up at me – an uninterested stare – and threw a smile at Fernandez. He half-smiled back, his eyes sweeping the room. Who was he looking for? A couple of men at different tables looked up. Then a large man in an open-necked shirt who'd been standing by the bar strode towards us, his arms wide, a huge smile on his face.

'Antonio!' He embraced Fernandez and the two men spoke in rapid Spanish which I couldn't follow. After a few moments I realised that they were talking about me.

Fernandez prodded the side of my head and chuckled. The other man looked sceptical, then laughed too.

'Hello, Ed,' he said, his accent thick and strong. 'I am Jorge. We see what you do, *vale*?'

'Vale,' I said. *Okay.* What else could I say? 'Ahora?' *Now?*

'No.' Jorge brushed his thinning hair off his forehead. 'After beer.' He turned and yelled across to the bar. 'Tres cervezas!'

61

We went over to one of the tables nearest the stage and sat down. A large mug of beer was placed in front of me. I took a few sips but felt too sick with worry to drink it properly. I don't really like the taste of alcohol anyway, if I'm honest – and certainly not beer.

How was I going to get out of this? Why was Fernandez even making me do it? I frowned, lost in my own thoughts as the clink of glasses and low murmur of voices faded away.

I'm not sure how much time passed. Eventually a man with a guitar dragged his chair to the front of the room and sang a song. It was slow and wailing and he was flat. Not that the rest of the bar seemed to care, they just carried on talking as if he wasn't even there. My spirits rose a little. Maybe no one would notice me after all.

Jorge ushered the singer off the stage, then came over to me. 'Ed?' he said.

Fernandez leaned over. 'Keep it simple,' he said. 'Don't cock it up.'

Legs shaking, I made my way to the stage. I sat in the chair the guitarist had vacated and looked up. Most people were still chatting away to each other, not paying me any attention. At least the lights were low. I glanced round, careful not to make eye contact with anyone. The woman in the pink top was watching me, nudging her neighbour, a thickset man with a streak of grey through his black hair.

He looked up, as Fernandez started speaking.

Fernandez's Spanish was fast, but I caught the occasional word. He was basically bigging me up, saying that I was able to do something extraordinary – *estupendo* … *maravillosa* – that the people watching wouldn't believe what I could do.

The room fell silent as he turned to me.

'You're up,' he said in a low voice.

'What d'you want me to do, exactly?' I hissed, my face burning.

'I told you.' Fernandez glanced round the room. 'Start with … I don't know – *him*, the man with the grey streak in his hair sitting next to that woman. Find something he doesn't want you to see, like you did with me.'

'No.' I stared at my hands, my heart thudding. I *couldn't* do this. Apart from anything else, it meant giving away the secret of my telepathy – the very thing we were here to protect.

'Do it *now*, Ed.' Fernandez lowered his head. I could feel his breath against my ear. 'If you don't read that man's mind in the next three seconds I will personally ensure that your three friends spend the rest of their time here in solitary confinement. Everything they *do* will earn them a demerit.'

I stared at him. *Surely* he couldn't mean that. Fernandez glared back at me, his eyes blazing. Instinctively, I knew that he *did* mean it. At this moment, he was prepared to do anything to make me perform. He had too much face to lose if I didn't. And it wasn't just *me*, if I didn't do what he said, Nico and Dylan and, worst of all, Ketty, would suffer.

There was no other option.

I looked into the audience. The man with the grey streak in

63

his hair was watching me, his mouth slightly open. I met his gaze. *Whoosh.* Seconds later I was inside his head.

The first emotion I felt was shock, then anger. But not at me. This was residual anger. His default emotion. I steadied my mind, waiting to catch a coherent thought.

Que pasa? What's happening? the man was thinking.

No te preoccupes. Don't worry, I thought back.

Around us I could hear raised voices. The woman beside him was speaking in a shrill voice. 'Manuel, Manuel,' she persisted. 'Mirame.' Look at me.

'Hurry up,' Fernandez hissed in my ear.

Manuel? I probed a little deeper. God, this man's head was a mess. Emotions and memories all muddled up ... indistinct thoughts careering round each other ...

A horse being whipped. Anger driving through everything.

I felt sick. I didn't like it. I swallowed, trying to find one coherent thought I could use. *There.* He kept thinking about someone called Susanna. A woman. He hated her, I was certain.

I broke the connection. Immediately, Manuel leaped to his feet, his fist clenched. He let out a stream of Spanish swear words, only a couple of which I recognised.

I stared down at the table. Fernandez gripped my shoulder. 'What did you see?'

The atmosphere in the room grew tense. Out of the corner of my eye I could see Manuel push back his chair. He advanced towards us.

'Ed,' Fernandez hissed. 'For God's sake.'

I looked up, not quite meeting his eyes. 'There's some woman called Susanna. He hates her.'

'La mujer Susanna,' Fernandez announced to the room. He turned to Manuel and spoke again in a burst of rapid Spanish I just about got the gist of. 'Why do you hate Susanna so much?'

Manuel stopped in his tracks. His furious face paled as he shifted his gaze from Fernandez to me. 'Por dios,' he said, sinking into the nearest chair.

For a split second there was silence, then Jorge tipped his head back and let out a roar of laughter.

'Su ex mujer, Susanna,' he shouted.

Fernandez clapped me on the back. 'Manuel's ex-wife,' he said. 'Well done, Ed, they know there's no way you could have known that.'

The room was buzzing now. Fernandez hushed the audience and made me mind-read several more people. In each case I felt their shock as they sensed my presence inside their heads, then a succession of thoughts in Spanish. Reading minds whose language I didn't understand was a completely different experience to anything I'd done before.

In a way it was easier to feel the basic emotions – the sense of the thoughts – without language cluttering the process up. On the other hand, that meant relying more on instinct than I was used to. I shook myself. What was I doing getting interested in the way my mind-reading worked?

At last Fernandez announced there would be a ten-minute

break. He sat down beside me at the table and signalled to the waitress to bring him a beer.

I sighed with relief and sank into my seat. Seconds later, Jorge appeared – beaming and ruddy-cheeked – at our table. He stood for a second, swaying slightly, then sat down in the chair in front of Fernandez. His beer slopped as he reached over and grabbed Fernandez' arm.

'Este increible!' he said, his speech slurred.

'Yeah, the boy's incredible.' Fernandez shook Jorge's arm off, clearly irritated.

Jorge didn't seem to notice. He was obviously extremely drunk. He launched into a rapid burst of Spanish. I just about caught the gist, despite his slurring, which seemed to keep coming back to the same point, over and over again, of how rich I was going to make him and Fernandez by pulling punters into the Casa Madelina every night.

I stared at Fernandez in horror. He couldn't possibly expect me to perform like this every night. Fernandez looked even more annoyed than he had earlier. He shook his head and told Jorge to calm down.

'No todos los noches,' he said. 'Algunas veces.'

Not every night. Every so often.

I sighed with relief. Well, that was something.

Jorge shrugged, unperturbed. He took a huge swig of beer, draining his mug, then thumped it down on the table and ordered three more.

'Me,' he said, turning to me with a huge grin. 'Try it me, the mind-reading.'

66

'Jorge, no!' Fernandez burst into a furious torrent of Spanish. He was speaking far too fast for me to follow now, but his meaning was clear.

I stared at the two men. Why was Fernandez so against my seeing what was inside Jorge's mind? He'd been happy enough for me to mind-read all these strangers.

With a jolt, I remembered the Escondite and the envelope containing those police reports. Was Jorge somehow involved in Fernandez's activities with the police van kids? It would make sense. After all, the two men were clearly working together to make money out of me.

Fernandez ended his outburst with a slap on the table that made the three beers that had just arrived splash onto the wooden surface.

'I'm going to the toilet,' he said to me. He shot Jorge a warning glance, then made his way through the crowded bar towards the exit.

Jorge made a face at his departing back, then took a huge gulp of beer. I tapped his arm and he turned, glassy-eyed, to face me.

'Quieres que leo tu pensamiento?' I said. *Do you want me to mind-read you?*

A sly look crept over Jorge's face. He grinned. 'Si, pero no es posible,' he slurred. 'I too fuerte ... strong ... it no work.'

'Okay,' I said, trying to hide my amusement at his drunken arrogance. Maybe I could use this to my advantage. 'Let's see.'

I met Jorge's unfocused gaze. *Whoosh.* I was inside his mind. It had a fairly light, easy-going, carefree feel, though

67

it was hard to distinguish one thought from another, presumably because of all the alcohol he'd drunk. I deliberately held back my own thoughts and feelings. Most people would still have registered my presence, but Jorge didn't seem aware of me inside his head at all. I took a moment to soak up his feelings – there was enthusiasm there ... greed ... a lust for life and enjoyment ... and, most pressing of all, a desire for more beer ...

Then I plunged in.

Donde esta el Escondite? Donde estan los ninos? I kept my thought-speech as light as possible. *Where is the Escondite? Where are the children?*

Jorge's conscious mind barely registered the question. I held my breath, sensing the answer drift drunkenly to the surface of his thoughts, then evaporate.

173 Calle Norte, San Juan.

My heart leaped. We were *in* San Juan. If the Escondite was here, then maybe so was Luz.

I broke the connection and looked at a spot just to the left of Jorge's nose.

He laughed. 'You see nothing,' he slurred. 'I knows. No es posible. No with me. You see nothing.'

I smiled. 'I see que quieres una cerveza,' I said. *I see you want a beer.*

Jorge roared with laughter. 'Always I wanting a beer,' he chuckled, slurping down another mouthful. 'You too. Drink.' He pushed one of the beer glasses towards me. I took a small sip. *Ugh.*

Across the room, Fernandez was making his way back towards us, a scowl on his face.

Jorge tapped the side of his nose. 'You say nada, Ed.'

'Nothing,' I agreed. 'I'll say nothing.'

As Fernandez reached us, Jorge stood up and pulled him into a huge hug. Fernandez disentangled himself with evident disgust, as two other men came over and started chatting to them both. I sat where I was, taking in what I'd seen in Jorge's mind. I could feel several people in the bar gazing at me and I closed my eyes, trying to block them out.

The room was stuffy and what little beer I'd drunk had given me a headache. Worse, I knew that in a moment Fernandez was going to ask me to do more mind-reading.

But at least now I knew where the Escondite was. And, surely, that *had* to be the place Fernandez was hiding Luz and the other police van kids?

'Ed.' Fernandez's voice cut through my thoughts. 'You're on again.'

I nodded. At least now I had a reason to perform ... to keep on performing. Somehow, I had to get out of this bar and find my way to 173 Calle Norte – and to Luz.

7: ESCAPE

Fernandez's mood improved dramatically on the drive home from Casa Madelina. He kept going on about how 'bowled over' everyone had been at my mind-reading performance, though I thought what he'd enjoyed the most was the wodge of euros Jorge had pressed into his hand before we left.

'Jorge was impressed too, the drunken idiot,' Fernandez went on. 'I've agreed we'll go back in a few days. Tell me, Ed, *how* do you do it?'

'I told you already,' I said, shortly. 'It's just a trick.'

It was pitch-black in camp when we arrived. Fernandez delivered me to my dorm and locked me in, with a warning to keep quiet about the evening, on pain of more solitary confinement and endless demerits. I found my bed in the dark and lay down, fully clothed. Across the room I could hear Mat and Mig's gentle snores and Tommy snuffling in his sleep. Seconds later Nico appeared beside me. I could just make out his face, pale in the gloom.

'Are you okay?' He sounded genuinely concerned. 'Ketty

was totally freaked out when Fernandez took you off earlier. Even Dylan looked worried when we told her.'

I explained where I'd gone and what Fernandez had made me do.

'It was humiliating,' I said. '*And* he threatened us all with solitary and non-stop demerits if I say anything to anyone – though, obviously, we *have* to tell Geri.'

'Yeah, well, we won't be able to do that for a while.' Nico sighed. 'Geri called while you were gone. She spoke to Dylan, but because Dylan had been in solitary all day she didn't know at that point that Fernandez had taken you off for the evening and she just went on about how horrible everything is here. You know what she's like. She's such a frigging princess, I think Geri thought she was overreacting. Anyway, Geri's not calling back for another two weeks.'

'*What?* But did Dylan tell Geri about the police van kids – and all that stuff I found in Fernandez's files?'

Nico shook his head. 'She said how we all think Fernandez is dodgy, but she was a bit vague on the specifics.'

I groaned. Why couldn't it have been me or Ketty who'd spoken to Geri?

'I've found out some more, as well.' I told Nico about the address for the Escondite I'd seen in Jorge's mind. 'I'm sure that's where Luz is,' I said. 'But I don't know how I'm going to get away from the bar long enough to find her.'

'Never mind finding *her* ...' Nico rolled his eyes. 'You *have* to find a way of calling Geri to get us out of here ... tell Fernandez you need breaks ... fresh air ... or somewhere to lie down, so you can slip out without anyone noticing.'

'Yeah, I will. There wasn't time tonight, though.' I paused. 'At least we know Geri will call again. Whoever speaks to her will be able to tell her everything, then. If she knew what Fernandez was making me do she'd have us out of here in five minutes flat.'

'Jesus, we could all be dead from frigging exhaustion in two weeks' time,' Nico said. 'Anyway, why didn't you tell any of the people you mind-read tonight that you needed to be rescued?'

I stared at him. 'I couldn't ... everything happened too fast and the people I mindread didn't really understand English ... Anyway, they would have just told Fernandez or Jorge ...' I tailed off. 'Maybe I can do both,' I said. 'Find Luz *and* a phone to call Geri on.'

Nico thumped the bed beside me. 'Forget this girl – whatever she's called – Loos,' he hissed.

'It's *Luz*,' I said, stubbornly. 'Like "Ruth", but with a "z" sound at the end.'

'Whatever, man.' Nico shook his head. 'Forget her. Getting us all out of here's the most important thing.'

I spent the next morning watering plants and picking green beans. Nico was digging up beds of earth in another part of the field and Ketty was indoors, but Dylan was in my group, along with Mat and Mig.

Thanks to the Spanish boys' poor English, it was easy enough for me and Dylan to talk quite freely about what

72

happened last night. I noticed that Dylan did half as much digging as the rest of us, lifting only light scatterings of earth and spending as much time as she could get away with leaning on her spade. Not that Mat and Mig were bothered. They seemed as in awe of Dylan as most of the boys at school were. I got that – I'd been in awe of Dylan myself once. She's kind of scary and beautiful at the same time. It's not just the basics – her long legs and hard green eyes. It's the way she holds herself. She's kind of like a cat – not belonging to anyone, ready to pounce at the slightest provocation. Anyway, she stood there, twisting her hair round her hand, while I told her what I'd found out – and what Nico had suggested.

'He's sooo right, Ed,' she said, scornfully. 'You have to forget this Luz person. And the others. Focus on getting the four of us out of here.'

I concentrated on tugging the next bean off its stalk. Why was I the only person who cared about the police van kids? Clearly the authorities didn't either, or Luz and the others wouldn't have been smuggled away to the Escondite.

Luz's sad face and huge eyes flashed into my head. I'd hidden the photo of her under my mattress where none of the others would find it and take the mickey. If only I could make remote telepathy work, then I could communicate with her directly. I felt depressed at the memory of my previous, failed, attempts. Still, maybe the fact that Luz was only in San Juan – and therefore a lot closer than my family back home – would help.

I'd give it a go as soon as I was alone.

'Are you listening to me, Chino Boy?' Dylan said.

I looked up. I hadn't even heard her. Dylan shook her head, then picked up a nearby trowel and pitched the tiniest amount of earth away from the bottom of the nearest bean stalk. 'You *have* to get to a phone next time.'

I opened my mouth to point out that Dylan had not exactly made the best use of her own phone call to Geri – but then didn't say anything.

After all, with Dylan, what was the point?

Fernandez appeared at breakfast. He made no mention of last night – didn't even speak to me directly – but he was in a good mood, joking and smiling with the Spanish kids.

Tommy was sitting next to Ketty when we went in. They'd been on kitchen duty together. But something was wrong. I sensed it before Ketty even turned to look at me. I went straight over and sat down opposite her.

'Hey, Ketty, what's up?' I smiled.

Ketty gave me a half-smile back. 'Nothing, just the normal crap of being here.'

That wasn't true, I was sure. Not for the first time I wondered why each of us had developed the particular gift we had. I'm sure that my Medusa gene developed into an ability to mind-read because I already have a strong intuition about when people are lying to me. It made sense too that outgoing Nico would be able to perform tele-kinesis, the showiest of psychic abilities, and that Dylan, the prickliest of our foursome, could protect herself from physical harm.

But when it came to Ketty, the connection wasn't so obvious. There wasn't really anything about her that explained why she should be able to see into the future. Not unless you counted her stubborn determination to see a task through once she'd started it . . .

'Did you see something?' I asked Ketty across the table. The question was vague enough for Tommy, who was still sitting next to Ketty, not to understand that I was really asking whether she'd had a vision of a future event.

Ketty shook her head. 'No, I haven't been able to "see" anything since we got here.' She looked across the room, out of the window. 'Too stressed, I guess.'

I nodded. Poor Ketty. After spending the past week or so building up her abilities, I knew it would be hard for her to feel out of control of her future-predicting skills now.

'Is that why you're upset?' I lowered my voice.

I sensed Tommy's gaze on me now, but kept my eyes fixed on Ketty. She shook her head.

I frowned.

'Ketts?'

She turned and looked me in the eye.

Whoosh.

My heart gave a jolt as I jumped into her mind. Of all the people I've ever mind-read, Ketty's is the hardest head for me to be inside. For a start there's my reluctance to be prying into her thoughts in the first place. Then my fear of

75

sensing her feelings about Nico. I mean, it's obvious how she feels about him – but I don't need it rammed down my throat. Most of all, I have to constantly be on guard with her so that she doesn't get a sense of *my* feelings for *her*. How much I like her – how the fact that we're best friends isn't quite enough, for me.

It's my birthday. Ketty's thought-speech rang in my head, loud and clear.

Oh. I wasn't expecting that.

Why didn't you say something? I thought-spoke back.

Ketty's emotions swirled near the surface. A confusing mix, quite unlike her mind the other times I've been inside it. I sat with her feelings, trying to sort them out. Frustration and misery were the strongest.

I'm sorry. I didn't know.

It isn't that – no one knows, not even Nico. There's no point. I mean, it's my birthday and I can't speak to Mum or Dad or Lex and there won't be any cake or presents or—

'Ed.' Nico's voice cut warningly across our thought-spoken exchange.

I broke the connection instantly and looked round.

Fernandez was standing in the doorway. He stared at me, an expression of curiosity on his face.

'Pass the jam, man,' Nico said, from down the table. Flustered, I did as he asked. Maybe Fernandez was going to call me over to talk about what happened last night. I turned round. But Fernandez had already gone.

*

76

The rest of the day passed quietly enough. I took Nico to one side and told him it was Ketty's birthday. Then he told Camila, while Tommy was listening. The two of them were on lunch duty and managed to concoct a makeshift birthday cake out of a handful of stale Swiss rolls with a twig for a pretend candle. We smuggled it outside during afternoon chores in the barn. Ketty loved it.

I didn't speak to Fernandez for the rest of that day, or the next two. Nothing much happened in camp – just the usual routine of chores and lessons – except during the morning of the second day, when a police van drove up while we were working in the field.

Cindy made us go inside so we couldn't see what – or who – was inside the van. Later, we were all sure we could hear noises coming from the barn, but Cindy and Don stood over us while we worked, so there was no way of sneaking over to take a look. I was certain the police van had brought more kids, presumably on their way to Escondite. It was deeply frustrating not being able to find out for sure.

Later that afternoon, a large car arrived and we were kept inside again. This time I managed to duck out of the kitchen, where I was on duty, to sneak a look out of one of the front windows. I caught sight of the tail end of a forlorn line of grubby kids being marched into the car. They drove off straight away and I'd only just made it back to the kitchen when Fernandez appeared and took me into his office.

'We're going back to the Madelina tonight,' he said. 'You don't have to do any more work this afternoon. Jorge says he's got quite a crowd coming to see you, so I want you fresh.'

The kids I'd seen earlier vanished from my mind. This was going to be my big chance to find Luz and get to a phone. I'd discounted by now the idea of asking for help telepathically. The Spaniards I was likely to encounter were going to be shocked enough to find me inside their heads. And even if I *could* somehow make them understand how we all needed rescuing, Fernandez would find some way of talking them out of it. I could just see him telling them I was delusional – or some kind of juvenile delinquent, like he had when I'd asked about Luz.

However, when we reached Casa Madelina, I quickly realised it was going to be impossible for me to get to a phone. Fernandez stuck to me like a bit of Velcro. When I went to the loo he even waited outside the cubicle. And though, this time, he did allow me breaks from the bar, I had to take them locked up inside an airless storage room. The only way to the deserted alleyway outside was through a locked, barred window. The bars were fairly rusty and, if I'd had Nico with me, we might have been able to pull them out through a combined effort of brute strength and telekinesis, but they were too much for me on my own.

We left the Madelina just before midnight. Fernandez, again, was in a great mood. I was exhausted.

'We'll be back in a few days,' Fernandez announced as we drove off in the dark.

'Right,' I said, feeling helpless. I remembered the rusty bars and the locked window. 'Er, I was wondering if I could take someone with me next time – another kid from Camp Felicidad – you know, to help with the performance side of things.'

Fernandez frowned. 'You mean like one of the Spanish girls, to help translate?'

'No,' I said quickly. 'Someone like Nico – someone who doesn't mind people looking at him.'

Fernandez's frown deepened. 'The kids you came with,' he said slowly. 'They know what you can do, don't they? I saw you and Ketty talking telepathically the other day. Can the others do your mind-reading trick too?'

'No,' I said, emphatically. 'No, they can't. They just know that I can. I just think, er, I'd feel better about what I was doing if I had a friend with me.'

It sounded pathetic. I stared at the floor, expecting Fernandez to laugh, but instead he murmured thoughtfully.

'Maybe it would make sense to have someone with you,' he said. 'But not Nico. One of the girls.'

I held my breath.

Fernandez slapped his hand on the desk. 'Dylan,' he said. 'She's the obvious choice.'

I stared at him. 'Dylan?' How was she going to be any help at getting hold of a phone to call Geri with?

'Yes.' Fernandez grinned. 'She's got the looks and the personality to help with the show. *And* her Spanish is better than the other two.'

This was true, though not what I wanted to hear. Given the

choice, Dylan was the last person I'd have taken with me. On the evidence of her digging efforts, I couldn't imagine she'd be strong enough to help pull out the bars on the window – and she was certainly unsympathetic to my concerns for Luz and the other kids.

But Dylan it was who, two days later, drove with us to San Juan.

We talked about it beforehand and she was confident she could find some way out of the bar.

'And once we're out on the street,' she insisted, 'we can *mug* someone for their cell phone if we have to.'

San Juan appeared as deserted as ever, but the Casa Madelina was heaving. The crowd was twice the size it had been last time. Most people were drunk, or getting there, and clearly having a good time. Dylan was immediately surrounded by men trying to get her attention.

Jorge stood at the back, happily drunk again. He whispered to me in broken English that he'd told a local journalist to blog about my mind-reading skills and the result was even more punters than before.

'Estupendo, eh?' Jorge said with a drunken grin.

I gritted my teeth. A bigger audience was the last thing I needed, but there was no time – or way – to explain this to Jorge.

Fernandez extricated Dylan from the men at the bar and beckoned me over to the front of the room. As I walked towards him, I noticed a tall thin man at the edge of the bar watching me intently. He gazed at me all through Fernandez's introduction, then melted into the crowd.

I did some mind-reading. It was nerve-wracking, but Dylan helped, doing most of the talking while I just looked up when instructed.

After three 'readings' I told Fernandez I had a headache and that Dylan and I needed to get out of the bar for a bit. He locked us in the storeroom I'd been in before.

As soon as we were on our own, we went over to the bars on the window.

'Maybe if we pull on these together?' I suggested.

Dylan whispered a countdown and we heaved at the bars. As I suspected, nothing shifted. After five or six goes, Dylan turned away in disgust.

'It doesn't matter, anyway,' I said, feeling dispirited. 'I'm sure the window behind is locked.'

'We're *not* letting this beat us.' Dylan's eyes flashed. 'Let's try again. That middle bar's a tiny bit wobbly. Come on.'

I put my hands on the bar next to hers. 'One ... two ... three ...'

I squeezed my eyes shut and yanked on the middle bar as hard as I could. To my amazement, it shifted, then came away in our hands.

'*Yes!*' Dylan whooped.

Five minutes later we'd managed to yank out the other two bars. My heart sank as I stared at the locked window that remained.

'If only Nico was here—'

'... he'd be no use whatsoever,' Dylan interrupted. 'This

81

window's swollen and stuck. No way could anyone open it, with or without telekinesis.'

'Then what can—?' I stopped as Dylan swung her fist back.

With a swift movement, she punched her arm through the glass. It broke, the shards smashing to the ground on the other side.

I raced to the door to see if anyone had heard. Music was still playing outside – a low rumble of drums and guitar drifting down from the bar. No yells or footsteps.

Dylan was now breaking off the shards of glass that remained in the window. She was using bare hands but her Medusa ability protected her from getting even the tiniest scratch. She finished, then glanced round at me and raised her eyebrows.

'No one's coming,' I whispered.

'Come on then.' Dylan already had her leg over the windowsill. 'Let's get out of here.'

Heart beating fast, I followed her up onto the chair and climbed outside.

8: THE CELLAR

As we ran down the street I wondered what Fernandez would do when he realised we were gone.

'How much time d'you think we've got before anyone starts looking for us?' I said.

'Not much.' Dylan scanned the road. There was no one else in sight. 'Come on, let's try down here.' She pointed down a street to the right and raced off. I followed, my heart thumping. We ran down several streets. I checked the names as we passed. *Calle San Pedro ... Camino de Vicente ... Calle de las Almendras ...*

Where was Calle Norte, the road that the Escondite was in?

Halfway down the next road, Dylan stopped. 'Where *is* everyone?'

We turned a corner and nearly banged into an elderly couple. Dylan immediately started clamouring in Spanish to borrow their phone, but the old man waved her angrily away and the couple scurried off.

We jogged on.

'Shit,' Dylan said as we turned the next corner. 'Suppose everyone refuses?'

'They won't,' I panted. 'Someone will help us.'

'Really, Chino Boy?' Dylan glanced at me contemptuously. 'And what makes you so freakin' sure of that?'

'Because people are basically good,' I said. 'They care about each other which—' I stopped in mid-sentence, my eye caught by the road name we were about to pass. It was painted on an old sign, tacked to a wall with rusty nails.

Calle Norte.

My heart leaped. 'Down here!' I said, running on before Dylan could stop me.

I pounded down the road, looking out for house numbers. There were a few stone cottages where I couldn't see any numbers, then suddenly there it was: 173 – a paint-chipped door next to a window with a red frame. I pushed at the door as Dylan panted up beside me. It was locked.

'What the freakin' hell are you *doing*?'

'I have to look in here. I think it's where Luz and those police van kids from the first day are being kept. You keep looking for a phone. If I see one in here, I'll call Geri myself.'

Dylan frowned. 'But—'

'It makes sense if we split up,' I said. 'Less chance of both of us getting caught.'

Dylan hesitated. I could tell she was torn between wanting to pour scorn on my latest suggestion and seeing the sense in it.

'Okay.' She pointed at the lock on the door. 'How are you going to get inside, though?'

I shrugged. 'Ring the doorbell?'

Dylan shook her head. She smashed her fist through the window next to the door, then reached round and clicked open the lock. The action had taken seconds and produced remarkably little noise.

'There you go. Make sure you find a freakin' phone and call Geri.' She rolled her eyes and ran off down the street.

I pushed open the door. The corridor inside was dank and gloomy. It smelled of damp. The glass from the window Dylan had broken had landed in a huge plant pot just inside the door. The earth must have cushioned its fall, which is why it had made hardly any sound.

I tiptoed inside, listening for anyone in the house.

Nothing.

I walked further down the corridor – it had a stone floor, and doors leading off it into empty, wood-panelled rooms on either side. At the end of the corridor were two wooden doors, both ajar. One opened into a brightly-lit room. I could hear the men inside talking in Spanish, their glasses clinking as they laughed at some joke. I pushed the other door further open. It led to a flight of stairs. Light from the hallway flooded the top steps, but I couldn't see where they ended. Voices floated up from the darkness beneath. I held my breath, straining to hear what was being said. I couldn't catch any words but the voices sounded fairly high-pitched ... children's voices.

I crept down the stairs. As I got closer to the bottom, a thin seam of light glowed under the heavy oak door opposite the final step. That was where the children's voices were coming from.

I tiptoed on. Sweat trickled down the back of my neck. The final stair creaked as I touched it. The voices on the other side of the door were suddenly silent.

I tugged at the large rusty door handle. This *had* to be the Escondite. Luz *must* be inside this room.

The handle resisted. Another locked door. For a second I wished Nico were with me. The thought reminded me of Dylan, outside somewhere – had she already reached a phone and called Geri? I'd pushed that part of my search to the back of my mind.

Small movements on the other side of the door. I took a deep breath and moved closer.

'Hola?' I whispered.

Silence on the other side. I wiped my hands on my chinos. Suppose I'd got it wrong? Suppose this was just some hang-out room for Fernandez's friends? Or other random men who weren't going to appreciate me barging in on their drinking or card-playing or whatever it was they were doing?

Well, I couldn't turn back now.

'Hola?' I said again.

'Hola.' A young voice on the other side. A boy.

'Soy Ed,' I said quickly. 'Por que estas aquí y los otros por aqui?'

More bad Spanish, but I couldn't think straight in my panic and at least that got my point across: *Why are you and the others here?*

The boy spoke so fast I couldn't follow exactly what he was saying at first, though I caught the word: *prisio ... prisoners*. I asked him to speak again, more slowly this time, which he did.

What I heard sent a chill right through me. From what I could understand, there were six children inside the room. They had come from various parts of the region and were all, as far as I could make out, in trouble with the police. They had originally been destined for some kind of detention centre, but the police had dumped them at Fernandez's camp, and they'd ended up here.

'The men say we are leaving in the morning, first thing,' the boy gabbled in Spanish.

'Estoy buscando una chica que se llama Luz,' I said. *I'm looking for a girl called Luz.*

'Quien?' *Who?*

I repeated her name. 'Do you know her?' I asked. 'Is she here?'

'No.' The boy's voice rose. 'Dejo aquí ayer.' *She left yesterday.*

My heart sank. I asked the boy if he knew where Luz had been taken.

The boy made a clicking sound with his tongue. 'No se,' he said. *I don't know*. He paused, then his voice grew pleading. 'Ayudanos, por favor.' *Help us, please.*

At that moment the cellar door above banged open. Footsteps stomped down the stairs. I shrank back into the shadows as a large man lumbered into view. He fished out

87

a key and undid the door. As he walked inside, I caught a glimpse of the room – it looked sparse, but cleaner than I'd expected. Two camp beds were pushed against the far wall. A row of scrawny kids sat on each one.

Jesus, what a place. And what were Fernandez and Jorge planning on doing with all these children?

I took advantage of the fact that the man was barking at the kids in Spanish, his back turned to me, to slip out of the shadows and race up the stairs. I listened at the top before creeping out into the corridor and along to the front door. The air was much fresher and cooler up here than down in the cellar. I glanced at the front door. Clearly no one had noticed the broken glass from the window beside the door yet. *Good.* That would make it easier for me to get away.

My spirits rose. I still hadn't managed to find Luz, but there was nothing more I could do for her right now. In fact, now I knew that children were definitely being taken to the house on the Calle Norte, the best thing I could do was turn the whole thing over to Geri. She could tell the authorities to investigate . . . to find Luz and save her . . . I just had to get to a phone.

I was about to gently twist the catch on the door and slip out, when footsteps sounded on the pavement outside. I ducked back behind the huge plant next to the door, my stomach twisting into knots.

And then the door opened and Jorge – the guy from the bar – appeared, a body slung over his shoulder. It was a girl, dressed in shorts and a halter-neck top, with long red hair falling down the sides of her face . . . Dylan.

Oh no. My breath caught in my throat as my brain took a few seconds to catch up with the evidence of my eyes. As Jorge disappeared down the corridor, puffing under the weight of his burden, I stared at Dylan's face. Her eyes were closed, her body hanging limp. She was unconscious.

Muttering a string of Spanish swear words, Jorge pulled open the cellar door I'd just emerged from, then stomped off down the steps, Dylan's head bumping against his back as he disappeared from view.

9: ANDREW STANLEY

I stood behind the flowerpot for several seconds, frozen with fear. What the hell did I do now? Panic ricocheted around my head. If Fernandez' men had caught Dylan, then Fernandez *must* himself be aware I was free by now – and be searching for me. What was I going to do? I felt sick as the image of Dylan's head bumping against Jorge's back flashed into my mind. She must have been attacked from behind, otherwise she'd have been able to stop the blows with her Medusa powers.

I had to get her out. I took a step across the hallway, then stopped.

It was crazy attempting to rescue Dylan by myself. I'd simply get myself trapped down in the cellar along with her. I thought it through. Dylan had been trying to find someone with a phone so she could call Geri to rescue us. That was the number one priority – everything else followed on from that. And I had to assume that Dylan had failed ... which left calling Geri up to me.

I turned on my heel and crept back to the front door. I sprang the catch and peered carefully outside. An old lady was shuffling along the pavement opposite. She glanced round at me with cloudy, unseeing eyes. I was willing to bet my life that she didn't carry a mobile phone. I glanced further up the road, towards the Madelina. That was the most likely direction Fernandez would appear from. I ran the opposite way, towards the crossroads about one hundred metres down. A car zoomed along the intersecting road as I ran. Then another. I'd flag one down if I had to. I gritted my teeth and raced on, slowing only slightly to cross a shadowy alleyway on my left. As I reached the other side, a tall, male figure strode out of the shadows, almost bumping into me.

He was wearing a suit. He was sure to have a phone.

I grabbed his arm, my heart pounding. 'Ayudame, por favor,' I said, the words suddenly tumbling out of me. *Help me, please.*

The man's eyes widened with surprise. He looked vaguely familiar. It took me a second to place him. Then I remembered. This was the tall, thin man I'd seen earlier at the back of the Madelina.

'Ayudame,' I said again. 'Telefono.' *Damn.* What was the word for 'borrow'? Dylan had used it earlier, but in my panic I couldn't remember.

The man smiled. 'I think we'll get on better if we speak in English,' he said smoothly. 'Now, what's the problem, kiddo? How can I help?'

I blinked, letting go of his arm. The man was English.

91

I swallowed, uncertain what to do. The man's smile seemed genuine, but I was in such a state I couldn't be sure he was really offering to help me. I stared at his face, half-tempted to mind-read him and make sure. His eyes were dark and intense, but I didn't get the sense he was hiding anything from me. What struck me more forcefully was how thin he was, the gauntness of his face accentuated by the way his dark hair was cropped close to his skull.

'Let me introduce myself.' The man held out his hand. 'I'm Andrew Stanley, European sales and marketing director for Electrical Security Solutions – here on business.'

'Ed.' I shook his hand, still feeling wary. I glanced over my shoulder. The street behind was empty.

'So, what are you running from, Ed?' the man said.

'Er ...' I hesitated, torn between my desire to ask for help and my anxiety about giving too much away. The obvious thing was to carry on with my original plan and ask this man if I could borrow his phone. And yet I'd seen him up at the Madelina. For all I knew he could be in league with Fernandez and Jorge. 'I saw you earlier, in the bar,' I said, scanning his face for any signs of guilt or complicity.

'That's right,' Stanley said evenly. 'I was on my way to Madrid, but my helicopter had to put down just outside San Juan because one of the instruments was faulty. My pilot's an excellent engineer but we won't be able to take off again until first thing tomorrow morning, so I thought I'd head out for a drink.'

'Right,' I said, my head spinning with all this new information.

'I remember what you did earlier,' he said. 'That's quite some mind-reading trick you've got going on. Does that have something to do with why you're running down this road like the furies are after you?'

'Sort of.' I glanced up and down the road again. The old lady had reached the end of the street and was turning the corner towards the Madelina. San Juan was not a huge town – Fernandez could be just a matter of minutes away. I looked back at Andrew Stanley. If everything he said was true, and it was surely too detailed to be made up, he was British, he was a professional and he was travelling by helicopter. He would almost certainly have a mobile phone on him. I *had* to ask for it. I didn't need to explain why I wanted it.

'May I borrow your phone?' I said.

Stanley raised his eyebrows. 'Sure, kiddo.' He fished a BlackBerry out of his pocket and peered at the screen. 'Damn it, there's no signal here. D'you want to come back to my hotel? I'm sure they'll have phones in the lobby you can use.'

I hesitated. Years of Mum warning me and my sisters not to follow strange men into cars and buildings were echoing in my ears. On the other hand, Stanley didn't seem like any kind of pervert. And I really, really needed to get away from the Escondite building before Fernandez appeared. Even Mum might appreciate the need to take a risk right now.

He held up his hands. 'Look, I'm just trying to help,' he said. 'There's obviously something very wrong here. I understand

93

that you're being cautious, but I'd really suggest that you come with me. I mean, you don't look like you should be out here on your own. Where are your parents? Have you got separated from them or something? Are they back at the bar?'

'No.' My guts twisted with anxiety. What had Geri said back in our training sessions? When you're lying, keep as close to the truth as possible. I decided to give Stanley my 'Ed Jones' cover story.

'I . . . we were sent to a camp – a brat camp sort of place – about two hours' drive from here,' I explained.

'We?' Stanley asked.

'There's four of us,' I explained. 'Friends who all arrived at the same time from England. But the camp isn't what it seems. The man who runs it is using it as a cover to smuggle kids in trouble with the law – like, really in trouble, not just annoying their parents – to a place called Escondite.' I pointed up the road. 'It's along there. Fernandez, who runs the camp, he's in league with the man who runs the Madelina where we were earlier. They're keeping the kids locked up, then they move them on somewhere else.' I thought of Luz, her huge, pleading eyes. 'I don't know where they go, but I'm sure it's bad, and now my friend Dylan's been taken there and I have to phone this woman I know back home who'll be able to help . . .'

'Jesus Christ, kiddo.' Stanley whistled, drawing me into the shadow of the alleyway. 'Never mind people back home. It sounds like we should call the local police.'

'There's no point.' As I spoke I could feel the tears bubbling up inside my throat. 'Fernandez and Jorge are working *with* the police. I think the police get some kind of kickback whenever they deliver a bunch of kids.'

I gazed up and down the road again. A couple appeared at the top of the street and started walking towards us.

Stanley hestitated. 'You really are in trouble,' he said. 'And so are those kids.'

'I know.' My voice cracked as I spoke. 'How far away is your hotel?'

'Couple of minutes' walk.' Stanley stood back, 'By the way, how come you haven't once looked me in the eyes while you've been speaking?'

I flushed. I wasn't used to people drawing attention to my dislike of making eye contact. Especially not complete strangers. I'd never had to explain it before, not that I could give Stanley the real reason, of course.

'Just makes me feel uncomfortable,' I stammered. 'I promise I'm not lying about any of what I've told you.'

'Okay.' Stanley's tone was suddenly brisk. 'So let's go and phone your mystery Saviour Lady back in England. See what she suggests we do.'

We walked swiftly down to the crossroads, turned left, then took a right almost immediately. A minute later Stanley stopped outside a stone house hung with a blue name plate: *Hotel San Juan*.

The reception area was very Spanish – all wooden furniture and ornate lanterns. A row of dolls in Flamenco dresses stood along the mantelpiece above the fireplace. Stanley spoke in rapid Spanish to the short, balding man behind the desk. His voice rose as he talked … he was clearly getting angry about something. The man behind the desk held up his hands as if to suggest the situation was not his fault.

'No, senor. Por la manana,' he said.

Stanley turned to me, exasperation in his eyes. 'Not only do I have no signal on my mobile, but the concierge here says some idiot drove a truck into the power lines just outside San Juan. All the phones are out till the morning – bloody useless country.'

Damn. How was I going to get help now? The boy I'd spoken to said the kids were being moved on first thing in the morning. I could feel tears pricking behind my eyes again. I shook myself. I had to be strong. The others were depending on me.

'Okay then.' I gritted my teeth. 'I have to go … walk to the next town … get to a phone that works …'

Stanley stared at me. 'No way, kiddo. The next town is miles away and the roads are unlit. You can stay here … make your call in the morning.'

I shook my head. 'I can't just do nothing. If I wait till morning all the kids at the Escondite – including Dylan – could be gone!'

There was a silence. Stanley narrowed his eyes thoughtfully, as if considering something. 'Well,' he said slowly. 'Maybe there *is* something we can do.'

'What d'you mean?' I asked, glancing over at the concierge.

He was looking curiously at us. Stanley clocked him and led me across the room, to a stiff brocade sofa.

'I'm thinking we should go into this Escondite place ourselves and make them release your friend, Dylan,' he said quietly.

I frowned. 'How will we do that?'

'Give me a moment to think it through.' Stanley paced across the room.

I sat down on the brocade sofa, wondering what argument could possibly work against Jorge and the Escondite guards.

After a couple of minutes, Stanley straightened his jacket and sat down beside me.

'Okay,' he said in a businesslike tone, 'let's work out what we're up against. How many guards d'you reckon there are at the Escondite?'

'At least three.' I frowned, trying to remember how many voices I'd heard through the door at the top of the stairs. 'Maybe more – and they don't look like people you can reason with.'

'Okay.' Stanley nodded. 'Then maybe rather than talking to them, we should try sneaking past, like you did before, and force open the door where these kids are being held. What was the lock like?'

'Big,' I said. 'And the door was massive, too. Made of oak, I think.'

'You noticed what it was made of?' he said.

'Yeah, my dad's a builder,' I said.

'Okay, so forcing the door isn't going to work – not without better tools.' Stanley paused. 'So it's back to plan A – we go in there and we ask them to release Dylan.'

I stared at him. 'What if they say "no" – or turn on us?' I said. 'Which I'm fairly certain they will.'

'Then we'll need backup.' Stanley grinned. 'And luckily I have something we can use.' He leaped to his feet. 'Come on, the stuff we need is in my room. I'll show you.'

What 'stuff'? I opened my mouth to ask, but Stanley was already storming up the stairs to the first floor of the hotel. I followed, feeling uneasy.

Stanley's room was two doors along. He unlocked the door.

'Come on in,' he said.

Oh, God. It was surely wrong for me to go into a strange man's hotel room. And yet, what choice did I have?

The room was neat and clean. A double bed dominated the space, covered with a crisp white sheet. An old wooden dresser stood in the corner. A door on the other side of the room led into a tiled bathroom. The window, opposite the bed, looked over the street we'd just walked up. Stanley crossed the room to where a row of small suitcases lay under the window. He pulled one out and flipped the lid open, revealing a row of plastic instruments. Some were short and and thin, others fatter and longer – like curved, plastic truncheons.

'What are they?' I said.

'Electronic Control Devices.' Stanley lifted one of the

larger instruments out of the case to show me. He pressed the trigger below the curve and electric sparks shot out of the end, together with a ratchety noise.

I jumped. 'You mean *stun* guns?' My mouth fell open. 'How come you're carrying a bunch of those in your luggage?'

'They're just part of the company's new range, The Lockdown 2000,' Stanley said, matter-of-factly. 'This is a demonstration pack I'm taking round the various offices to show while I visit.' He grinned at me. 'It's what we do ... my company ... E.S.S. Electrical Security Solutions. We provide the whole package – alarms, hidden cameras, weaponry. Here, try one.' He chucked me one of the smaller Lockdown models.

I pressed the trigger. Sparks flew out of the end. The Lockdown juddered in my hand. 'Wow,' I said. 'Er ... how come you're prepared to help me like this?'

Stanley shrugged. 'I don't know, it just feels like the right thing to do.' He paused, turning away from me, towards the window. 'My wife and I can't have children. She – Sandra – she has this attitude that whenever we come across kids who need our help we should try and help them. It's just a way of giving something back, when we can't be parents ourselves.'

I nodded. Sandra was my stepmum's name. It seemed like a good omen.

Stanley carefully shut the Lockdown suitcase, then turned to me, his expression very serious.

'Remember, these are proper weapons. We only use them if we have to. Okay?'

I nodded, my head spinning. 'What ... er, how do we use them – if we have to?'

'It's simple. You just have to get right next to the person you want to disable, then press your Lockdown against his torso. The back or chest is ideal, but anywhere will do. Avoid the face though – we want to knock them out for a few minutes, not cause lasting damage.' He shot me a grim smile. 'I might trade in electronic guns but I'm no vigilante.'

I stared at him, completely lost for words.

'You okay with this, kiddo?' Stanley said.

I nodded, not sure I could speak. I pressed the Lockdown again. I had to admit, it made me feel powerful.

'What's the plan?' I said.

'What do *you* think we should do?'

'Er ...' I thought for a second. 'Get inside the Escondite. Knock out the guards if they won't listen to reason. Find their keys. Lock them in a room, then release everyone from the cellar.'

'Sounds good.' Stanley nodded. 'What about that mind-reading trick of yours? It's pretty impressive – you could perform at the Palladium.' He laughed. 'Can you see any way of making use of that?'

'Not really.' I considered it for a moment. 'We already know where we're going.'

'You can't somehow work out what they're doing right now? Tap into their thoughts at a distance?'

'No,' I said, thinking about my recent failed attempt at connecting with Mum and Dad via remote telepathy.

'Okay.' Stanley shoved his Lockdown inside his jacket pocket. 'Then let's go.'

10: FINDING DYLAN

Someone, I reckoned, was bound to have boarded up the window Dylan had smashed earlier. According to Stanley, it didn't matter.

'If we ring on the doorbell, chances are just one person will come,' he said as we walked up the road, our Lockdowns in our pockets. 'The guards will be easier to deal with one by one – both the talking and, if it comes to it, the fighting.'

I glanced sideways at him. His nose was slightly pointed at the end, I noticed, and his forehead permanently creased with a vertical line. His thin, angular face had the look of a fox about it, or maybe a wolf. But there was no fear in his eyes.

In fact, considering what we about to do, he seemed amazingly calm.

'How do you know about … er, the fighting side of things?' I asked.

'Five years in the army,' Stanley said, matter-of-factly. 'I only went into sales and marketing because my wife said if I didn't leave the forces, she'd leave me.'

'D'you miss it?' I asked.

'All the time.' Stanley sighed. 'I still get to travel and I spend time in the T.A. as well – that's a volunteer army organisation.' Stanley shot me a look. 'You should try it. That is, you should sign up for the Combined Cadet Force. All boys should.'

I looked down the road. It was past 2 a.m. and very dark. The stars were out overhead, but the moon was a thin crescent and the street lights spread far apart down the street.

'I don't think the army's really my thing,' I said. 'Not that I know what "my thing" is.'

Stanley nodded. 'Well, I'm sure you'll work it out – all in good time. Like I said, that mind-reading trick you can do could make you big bucks, if you wanted.' He paused. 'Hey, what's the secret? How do you do it?'

Oh God. Why did he keep going on about it? For a second I almost panicked. Then I took a deep breath. I didn't need to answer the question. That was another tip Geri had given back at Fox Academy. *Head off unwanted questions with a distraction, ideally a humorous one.*

'If I told you, I'd have to kill you,' I said, attempting a grin.

I wasn't sure I'd pulled off the humour but, to my relief, Stanley laughed.

'Fair enough,' he said. 'Well, if we rescue your friend, maybe you can tell me later.'

We walked the last few metres up to the Escondite in silence. As I expected, the window had already been boarded over. Stanley glanced at me. 'Lockdown ready?' he said.

I nodded, my throat suddenly dry.

Stanley pressed the doorbell then stood back away from the door, out of sight. I waited, my heart in my mouth, as footsteps echoed along the corridor. Heavy steps. They stopped. There was a moment's pause, while whoever was on the other side of the door presumably looked through the eyehole and saw me. A loud grunt, then the sound of a bolt being scraped back.

The door swung open. It was the guard I'd seen earlier.

Stanley spoke in Spanish. I couldn't catch every word, but he was basically asking about the children downstairs. As soon as he said the word for prisoners – *prisioneros* – the guard drew a gun from his jacket.

I gasped. In a split second, Stanley darted forward and shoved his Lockdown against the man's chest.

The guard staggered, then fell forwards. Stanley caught his weight and laid him quietly on the tiled hallway floor.

Oh my God, oh my God.

My breathing was coming out in shallow gasps ... my heart racing. I backed against the wall. Stanley looked up at me, his eyes glinting in the dim light.

'I don't think talking's an option, Ed,' he whispered.

We stared at each other. I still couldn't breathe properly ... couldn't think ...

Stanley stood up. 'It's okay, Ed,' he whispered. 'Everything's going to be okay, but we need to get going before the other guards realise we're here – or this one wakes up. Now shut the front door. Quietly.'

I nodded, closing the door as gently as I could. My hands were trembling.

'Good,' Stanley whispered. 'Which way to the kids?'

I pointed to the stairs. We crept along the corridor towards them. As we passed the door behind which I'd heard adult voices earlier, a man inside yelled out.

'Que pasa, Enrique?'

He was obviously calling for the guard Stanley had hit with his stun gun.

I glanced at Stanley. He was staring at me, his expression intent. He held up his hand, one finger pointing towards the door, then raised his eyebrows.

I knew he was asking me if I was ready to burst in and knock the remaining guards out. I nodded, still feeling dazed, and pulled my Lockdown out of my pocket.

I held my breath, waiting. Then Stanley shoved the door open and everything seemed to happen at once.

Stanley rushed into the room. I ran in behind him. There were three guards inside. One on his feet, already walking towards us. Stanley jabbed towards him, thrusting the Lockdown at his shoulder. I heard the ratchety noise and the subsequent thud as I turned towards the two men at the table in the middle of the room. I had a dim impression of a card game and a bottle of beer. The man nearest me was reaching towards his pocket. For a gun? I didn't stop to think about it. I leaped forwards, Lockdown outstretched, and pushed the weapon against the man's chest. Sparks shot out. The man's eyes glazed over. He fell back, with a thud, into his chair.

105

Behind me I could hear the same sequence of sounds repeated as Stanley dealt with the third guard.

The whole thing had taken less than ten seconds.

'Find the keys,' Stanley barked.

Panting, I reached inside my guard's jacket. A bunch of keys bulged in his pocket. I took them out and we raced to the door. We dragged the guard Stanley had knocked out earlier into the room, removed all phones and guns, which Stanley placed by the front door, then locked the men in.

'So far so good,' Stanley muttered. 'Now, where's this cellar?'

We made our way down the stairs. There was silence inside the room. As Stanley fumbled with the keys, trying one after another in the lock, my heart beat a loud drum roll against my throat. Suppose all the kids inside were gone already?

It seemed to take forever, but it could only have been a few seconds before the door opened and I raced inside. A single light bulb swung from the ceiling, casting an array of eerie shadows around the room. I looked over at the kids, most of whom were huddled together on the two camp beds, as they started to stir. A short boy with tufty hair stared sleepily at me.

'Ed?' he said.

It was the boy I'd spoken to earlier, on the other side of the door.

'Si.' I looked round. There were six kids here. Two boys

and four girls. None of them looked older than eleven. There was no sign of Dylan.

'Donde esta la chica con el pelo rojo?' I asked, hoping Dylan's distinctive red hair would have marked her out.

'Ha salido.' There was a finality to the boy's tone I didn't like.

'Gone where?' In my haste I forgot to speak in Spanish.

The boy stared stupidly at me. One of the girls started speaking in a rapid, high-pitched Spanish I couldn't follow.

I turned to Stanley, who was watching all this intently.

'What's she saying?' I asked.

'The girl with red hair has gone with the other big girls, to the Casa Elena,' he translated. 'It's a place where people come to find cheap labour – you know, housemaids and cleaners and so forth. This girl heard the guards talking about it. Apparently there were arguments. Someone called Jorge wanted to sell her on, but your guy Fernandez insisted she should stay here until he'd found you – then he's taking her back to his camp.'

I nodded. That made sense. As far as Fernandez was concerned, Dylan had wealthy parents expecting her home at some point. She was worth far more to him in camp, than out of it, though clearly Jorge had disobeyed his orders to leave her here while he looked for me.

'Where's Casa Elena?' I said.

'I don't know. This girl says it's in San Juan, though, which is something.' Stanley paused. 'We need to get these kids to a safe place, then we can look for her.'

I nodded. 'Venga,' I said to the first boy. *Come.*

The six kids obediently followed Stanley and me out of the cellar and up the stairs. Once we were outside and on the street, Stanley spoke again to the girl who'd told us about Dylan and the Casa Elena.

'These kids have been fed and allowed to wash,' he said to me quietly. 'Doesn't look like they've been physically harmed. My guess is that Fernandez and Jorge are planning to sell them on as slave labour, like the older girls, but in factories rather than households.'

My mouth fell open. 'That's terrible. Surely they wouldn't get away with that?'

Stanley gave a tired shrug. 'It happens all over the world. Street urchins like these ... no families to speak of ... in constant trouble with the law ... Throw in a few corrupt police officers, an overworked social services system and one or two entrepreneurial bastards like Fernandez prepared to take risks to make some extra bucks – and it's all too easy to see how it happens.'

As we emerged onto the darkness of the Calle Norte, I fell silent. Home, and Mum and Dad and my sisters and our simple routines – meals, TV, school etc. – seemed a million miles away. I looked round at the kids. They were still all huddled together, looking up at us with wide, frightened eyes.

'*Ed?*' It was Stanley.

I started, not realising he'd been speaking to me.

'I was saying that there's a convent just down the road

108

from my hotel. We can leave the kids there. Possibly the nuns will also have heard of Casa Elena. It's hard to keep secrets in small towns.'

'Okay.' My guts twisted into a painful knot as I remembered Luz. I was sure Dylan would be safe. Fernandez was too smart to let anything really bad happen to her. Anyway, I couldn't imagine Dylan as anyone's housemaid. But what about Luz? She was, presumably, at the Casa Elena too, waiting to be sold on to some exploitative family.

The nuns at the convent looked shocked when we turned up in the middle of the night with all the street kids in tow. It took a few minutes for Stanley to explain what had happened, but once they understood, the nuns readily agreed not only to take the kids, but to contact the police in Madrid in the morning.

'They'll help track down the children's real families, if there are any,' Stanley explained as we left. 'At the very least, they'll be put into proper care homes.'

'Suppose the homes aren't nice places?' I said.

Stanley shook his head wearily. 'There's nothing we can do about that. At least these kids won't be sold into slavery now.'

I supposed that was true, though it was hard to leave all those frightened children at the mercy of a State which had already failed them once. Again I thought of home and my sisters. Kim was only nine. About the same age as many of these street kids. Still, what else could we do? I could hardly start trying to find families for every child myself.

'We deal with what we can, Ed,' Stanley said, seemingly guessing my thoughts. 'I'm trying to help you because it's the right thing to do, but you have to know where to draw the line – where to hand over to the professionals.'

I sighed. I knew he was right, but it still didn't feel good.

We headed for Casa Elena. The nuns at the convent had heard of the place – apparently it had once been a bar, but the Madelina had put it out of business.

'As far as the nuns are concerned it's empty,' Stanley explained as we walked along another deserted San Juan street. 'They say it's really run-down.'

They weren't lying. Casa Elena was little more than a shack, complete with a rickety wooden porch and paint-peeled windows. The whole place was in darkness. Stanley fished his Lockdown out of his pocket and glanced at me. 'Ready?'

'Yes.'

Stanley knocked on the door.

A sleepy female voice answered in Spanish. 'Quien es?' *Who is it?*

'Senor Fernandez.' Stanley lied, his voice low and insistent. 'Abre la puerta.'

Seconds later, the door creaked open. An elderly woman dressed in a long white nightgown stood in front of us. Her mouth fell open as she registered Stanley was not Fernandez. Before she could call out, he darted forward and pressed his Lockdown against her shoulder. He held it there for a few seconds after she collapsed. I stood there, shocked – had that

110

really been necessary? She wasn't exactly going to fight us . . .

'She'll be out for a while now,' Stanley said, matter-of-factly, dragging her inside. I followed him, feeling troubled. Despite the late hour, the house was swelteringly hot. The front door opened into a smelly, open-plan room with a TV and a tatty sofa at one end and a grimy kitchen area at the other. There was no sign of any one else around.

I glanced at the stairs in the corner. 'The girls must be up there,' I whispered.

Stanley laid the old woman in a chair and straightened up. 'Let's go,' he said.

We crept up the stairs. Every step creaked, but there was no sound from the landing. It was tiny, with only three doors – one of which stood open, revealing the outline of bathroom furniture. Stanley twisted the handle of the room next door and pushed it silently open. A bedroom – with one large double bed, a mess of clothes . . . and nothing else. It was empty.

He signalled across to the remaining room. The door was shut. I tried the handle. Locked. I was sure we could break it down between us – it looked as rickety as the rest of the house.

Stanley clearly had the same idea. He mimed shoulder-barging the door. I nodded, and he held his hand with three fingers pointing up. One down. Two down. Three down. As he made a fist, we both stood sideways on to the door and shoved against it.

It splintered easily and we burst together into the room. Darkness. Then a light from the other side of the room flashed into our eyes. A smash. Something broke over Stanley's head. He let out a groan. Blinded by the glare of the light, I darted forward and shoved my Lockdown in the direction of the attacker. Contact. I had no idea whether my weapon was pressed against a person or a piece of furniture. I pressed the trigger anyway. Sparks. A thud as someone fell to the floor I knelt and held the stun gun against them for a couple more seconds, determined to make sure they were completely unconscious. The light across the room dipped. A squeal – a girl's voice.

I looked in the direction of the light. I could just make out a lamp held in someone's hands ... the outline of a girl.

Luz.

Forgetting Stanley and our unconscious attacker, I raced towards her. As she recognised me, her eyes grew wide.

'Eds, English,' she said softly. 'You come.'

'Si,' I said.

My stomach was doing cartwheels at the sight of her. She was more amazing-looking even than I'd remembered. I could feel my face blushing bright red. She was staring at me ... and it wasn't like with anyone else, ever ... I just *had* to meet her eyes. I couldn't stop myself. They were so beautiful – huge, and shining with sudden gratitude in the lamplight.

Whoosh. I was inside her head. This time, she was expecting it. I took a second to register the 'feel' of her mind.

I sensed a huge amount of fear, but also a strong sense of survival and a steady quality that I wasn't used to in people our age.

Hola, Luz, I thought-spoke, trying to calm my own thoughts and feelings which were jumping around like rabbits.

Hola, Eds. How do you this?

'Ed.' Stanley's voice beside me brought me back to the present.

I broke the connection with Luz. 'Are you okay?' I asked him.

'Yes, but I'm not so sure about this girl you knocked out.' Stanley pointed to the shattered remains of a vase which lay on the floor at his feet. Beside the broken vase was a girl with red hair.

My heart leaped into my mouth. It was Dylan.

She wasn't moving.

11: HELICOPTER RIDE

I stared at Dylan's body. Had I killed her? No, I'd only used a stun gun, even if I had been pressing hard on the trigger for a good three or four seconds after she'd fallen. Surely she was all right? Stanley hauled her to her feet. Her head lolled and her arms hung limply by her side.

'Oh God,' I groaned.

'She'll be fine, kiddo,' Stanley insisted.

As if in confirmation, Dylan let out a low moan. I sighed with relief.

Luz was tugging on my arm. 'La chica, your friend ...' She lapsed into a stream of Spanish I couldn't follow.

Stanley nodded. 'This girl says that Dylan thought we were the old woman. Apparently, earlier, she tried to attack the old lady so they could get away, but the old lady hit her back.' He paused. 'The girl says she doesn't understand how, but somehow Dylan wasn't hurt – she only pretended to be – and was waiting by the door, hoping for another chance to attack her.'

I nodded. That sounded like Dylan successfully deploying her defence-against-physical-harm ability.

'She's definitely going to be okay?' I said.

'You held that stun gun against her for a while too long, kiddo. But she'll be fine, yes. She'll be out for a bit, then she'll probably want to sleep it off for a few hours.' Stanley hauled Dylan over his shoulder. 'Come on. We need to get out of here before Fernandez works out where we are.'

He turned to leave. I touched Luz's arm. 'Ven,' I said gently. 'Come with us.'

'I don't think so,' Stanley said from the door. 'We can't take on any more people, we've got to get to this camp and find your other two friends.'

I stared at him. He hadn't mentioned rescuing Nico and Ketty before.

Luz shuffled closer to me. I was pretty sure she hadn't understood Stanley's exact words, but she had certainly got the gist of his argument.

'We can't leave Luz here,' I said, my heart beating fast.

'I'm not saying that,' Stanley said, impatiently. 'We'll tell her where the convent is. She's old enough to make her own way there and explain herself to the nuns.'

'No.' I don't know what made me so bold. I was really in no position to argue with Stanley. He had already gone way out of his way to help me – and he'd just implied he was prepared to go even further and, somehow, take us back to Camp Felicidad to rescue Nico and Ketty.

'*No?*' Stanley's eyes widened. He adjusted his hold on Dylan's legs.

'No, it's not fair. She's got no one else. And it's the middle of the night.' I stared defiantly at Stanley. My heart pounded. Luz's slender arm pressed against mine. She was trembling. I put my arm round her shoulders.

'But, Ed ...'

'I promised I would help her.' This was true – and I already had a plan for making it happen. I was sure that once I'd explained Luz's situation to Geri, she'd be willing to help find her a proper home. 'Anyway, she's only one more person and I'm *not* leaving her behind.'

Stanley hesitated for a second, then exhaled slowly. 'Fine,' he said. 'But come on, we need to hurry and your friend here isn't getting any lighter.'

We made our way swiftly out of the house. Outside it was almost light – the sky a beautiful rose-tinted orange colour, glinting on the horizon where the sun was about to rise.

A short time later, we arrived back at Stanley's hotel. He deposited Dylan in an armchair in the lobby and told us to wait while he raced upstairs to collect his bags. A couple of minutes later he was back, barking out orders in Spanish to the concierge who'd been giving Luz, the still unconscious Dylan and myself some very odd looks.

Stanley asked the man to sort out a taxi, then slipped him some money, pointing at us then miming the zipping up of his mouth to indicate the need for absolute silence.

My head spun as I watched him. Sitting down for the first

time in hours I realised how tired I was. What a relief that I'd run into Stanley ... that he was looking after us like this, prepared to go to such lengths to help.

The concierge vanished and Stanley came over to us.

'If there's a signal now I'd like to call Geri,' I said. 'Tell her what's going on.'

Stanley fished out his BlackBerry. 'Signal's still dead,' he said. 'The concierge says all the main lines are still down too. He's just gone next door to raise his brother to take us to my helicopter.'

I sat back, feeling uneasy. But there wasn't time to think. A few seconds later the concierge was back, accompanied by a short bald man who looked just like him.

'Let's go,' Stanley said, hauling Dylan to her feet again. 'Goldie's waiting for us at the helicopter. We need to get to your camp before Fernandez realises what's going on. If we can arrive before everyone's up, we'll be able to launch a sur-prise attack on the camp, get your friends out fast and clean.'

As I carried his suitcases to the taxi, the question that had been building up in my mind forced its way out.

'Why are you doing all this?' I said. 'I mean, rescuing Dylan and Luz was one thing, but the camp's miles away – what about all your business work?'

Stanley placed Dylan carefully in the back of the cab, then got in the front. As Luz and I settled ourselves in the back and the taxi set off, Stanley turned to face me.

'I told you last night, it just feels like the right thing to do. Sandra and I agreed that if a child came our way in need of help, it was our duty to step up to the plate. Plus, if I'm honest, it's also a buzz.' He grinned. 'Like I told you, I miss the army – and it'd be a shame to let that combat training go to waste, eh, kiddo?'

I nodded, still not entirely convinced. Something wasn't quite right here, though I couldn't see what. After all, Stanley had done nothing but help me so far. My dad was always saying that people were basically good – and just needed the opportunity to work hard to make the most of their potential.

On the other hand, Mum always said that beliefs like that explained why other people were rich and Dad was still a struggling builder who couldn't afford to replace our ancient, battered Ford Fiesta.

The helicopter was waiting for us at the edge of town. As we reached it, a red-haired man in jeans and a stained, greasy top emerged from the hut nearby. He grinned as we all got out of the taxi, revealing a gold front tooth.

'This is Goldie,' Stanley said. 'My pilot.' He jerked his thumb at the boot and Goldie retrieved the suitcases.

We helped pull Dylan out of the taxi and set her down in the shade of the nearby hut.

'We leave in five minutes,' Stanley said. 'There's a toilet in the hut if anyone needs to go.' He repeated this in Spanish for Luz. She went inside immediately.

I sat down next to Dylan as her eyes flickered open. She raised her hand to her head and gave a moan as she rubbed her forehead.

'Jesus, what happened?' she grunted.

'You okay, Dylan?' I said, sitting beside her.

'Yeah, freakin' fantastic,' she snapped, her eyes coming properly into focus. 'Where am I?'

'Still in San Juan. We, er ... we rescued you and Luz and now we're waiting for a helicopter ride out of here,' I said. 'This man, Andrew Stanley, he's helping us get to the camp so we can get Nico and Ketty.'

Dylan rubbed her head again. 'Why don't we just call Geri – or the police?'

'There's no signal to call out from round here – and the local police won't move against Fernandez – they all knew about that Escondite place – the whole scam.'

Dylan nodded, then yawned. 'I can hardly keep my eyes open.'

'Stanley said that you would – he said that's what it's like after ... after what happened to you.' I was in no hurry to admit to Dylan that I was the one who had knocked her out.

'So why are those two men helping us?' Dylan said, trying to repress another yawn.

I looked over at Goldie and Stanley, deep in conversation by the helicopter.

'I don't really know,' I admitted. 'I guess they're just good people.'

Dylan gave a contemptuous snort and slumped back against the wall. Seconds later her breathing grew shallow and even. She was clearly asleep.

Stanley beckoned me over. He laid a large map of the area on the ground and pointed at a spot to the west of San Juan.

'This is where we are now.' He waved his hand across the desert beyond San Juan on the map. 'Where d'you think your camp is?'

I studied the map. I've always like orienteering and I know how to read maps well. A range of mountains ran to the north of the town we were in. I distinctly remembered seeing the sun setting to the right of those, which meant that when Fernandez and I had driven towards San Juan from Camp Felicidad, we must have been journeying southwards. I pointed to the desert area above San Juan on the map.

'The camp's here somewhere. Due north of the town – as far away as it would take a jeep travelling at about fifty miles an hour to do the journey in two hours, so . . .' I thought for a second, 'roughly one hundred miles north of San Juan.'

Stanley smiled. 'Well done, kiddo.'

A few minutes later we were all in the helicopter. Dylan grumbled as we woke her to make her get on board. She sat right at the back and fell asleep again immediately, her head wedged against the window. Luz huddled close to me in the row in front. I put my arm round her again as Goldie and Stanley got in behind the controls. I was anxious about what lay ahead. It wouldn't be easy to liberate Nico and Ketty from the camp, but on the other hand we were here with two adults – one of whom certainly knew how to handle himself – and with the resources to make an easy and speedy getaway.

I didn't know anything about helicopters, but this was a smart one. There was a spare seat beside me and Luz, and two behind us, next to Dylan. I wondered idly why Stanley needed such a capacious machine when all he was travelling with were a couple of suitcases, but then Luz snuggled closer to me, laying her head on my chest, and everything else went out of my mind.

She smiled up at me, her eyes glinting sea-green in the dim light. As the helicopter engine started and the blades whirred above us, she said something in Spanish. The noise was too great for me to follow exactly what she said, but I caught the words *tu corazon* and *muy rapido*.

I blushed. My heart was certainly beating very fast and not entirely, if I was honest, because we were about to set off on a dangerous rescue mission. I bent my face closer to hers. I had no idea what to say . . . still, the way Luz was looking at me, maybe I didn't need to say anything at all.

And then the helicopter gave a lurch and we were off, rising into the air.

My stomach rose into my throat as we swooped down and rose again. All thoughts of kissing Luz deserted me as overwhelming fear and a strong desire to vomit took their place.

Luz seemed to sense my anxiety. She patted my arm and pulled away from me.

'No te preoccupes, Eds,' she said.

Don't worry.

I swallowed and closed my eyes. I'd felt sick on my last helicopter ride, when Nico and I had gone to Cornwall to rescue Ketty. She was being used as bait to lure us into a trap, so that we could be handed over to a weapons dealer called Blake Carson.

Carson himself was planning to sell us on to military out-fits in other countries, to use – or misuse – our abilities for their own ends. Luckily Nico and Ketty had saved us that day – and the police had arrested Carson.

Well, today I would repay the favour. Today it was Nico and Ketty's turn to be rescued.

12: THE RESCUE

I felt sick for the whole helicopter ride. Luz, on the other hand, seemed to be loving the experience. She shuffled across a seat so that she could look properly out of the window and made constant exclamations in Spanish. Stanley had explained to her by now that once we had rescued Nico and Ketty he would take her to a safe place where the process of tracking down any remaining family could begin.

She'd explained to me that both her parents were dead – that she'd been in and out of a number of care homes, getting in trouble with the police for various minor incidents. She thought her aunt and her grandmother lived in Toledo, and was eager to try to reach them.

'Maybe I go live with them, Eds,' she'd said eagerly.

I couldn't see this as a very likely outcome. After all, if they'd wanted to take her in why hadn't they done so after her parents died? Still, I supposed it was worth a try.

Luz asked me about my telepathy on the flight. Fighting

my nausea, I explained in extremely limited Spanish that it was just an ability I'd been born with and that I didn't like to use it too much. Luz looked bemused, but accepted what I said, turning back to the window to gaze out in wonder at the town spread out beneath us.

As the journey went on, she told me more about her life. How she'd never known her dad, how her mum and older brother had been drug addicts, how she'd lived rough after they died before being picked up by the police. Her story, told partly in Spanish and partly in broken, stumbling English, transfixed me. I'd never met anyone who'd gone through half as much. I mean, all of us with the Medusa gene had to live with the knowledge it had killed our mothers – and I was the only one who actually knew his real father. But that was *nothing* compared to Luz's experiences.

I'm not sure how long we were in the air, but the sun was well up in the sky when Luz clamoured excitedly that she'd seen a building that looked like the camp. Dylan, I noticed, was still sleeping soundly, so with a great effort I turned my head and identified it as Camp Felicidad.

We banked swiftly and zoomed towards it. Goldie lowered the helicopter several hundred metres away, behind a sandy hillock. It couldn't be seen from the camp there, though anyone watching would have certainly noticed it land. However, according to Stanley's watch it was now almost 5 a.m., which meant no one would be up yet to notice anything.

124

'Tell me about the camp,' Stanley said.

I explained quickly how it was laid out and where the male and female sleeping areas were. 'I don't know where Fernandez, Cindy and Don sleep, though,' I admitted. 'They must be somewhere in the main building.'

'Not to worry.' Stanley patted the Lockdown in his pocket. 'There's no way Fernandez will be here yet – he still thinks you're on the run from him in San Juan and will be looking for you there. All we have to worry about are two adults who are a) probably asleep and b) unaware we're here. They might be armed, of course, but so are we.'

I felt for my own Lockdown. I didn't want to have to use it again, not after what I'd done to Dylan. But at least I knew I could if I had to. I smiled. 'This'll be our third rescue mission in as many hours,' I said.

'Yes, and potentially the most risky.' Stanley didn't smile back. 'So keep your wits about you.'

After a short deliberation, Stanley left Goldie, Luz and the still-sleeping Dylan with the helicopter.

'Best if we keep the gung-ho factor to a minimum, kiddo,' Stanley said. 'If we take too many people, there's more risk of accidental noise. Plus,' he smiled at me, 'I know *you* know how to handle one of those.' He pointed to my Lockdown.

We set off across the desert, the dawn air chilly against our faces. Our plan was to creep up on the camp, using the barn on the side as cover. We would break one of the windows to get into the main building, find Ketty, then move on to the outhouse dorm where Nico slept.

125

The first part of this went as smoothly as it could have done. Stanley broke the window with a speed and a style that even Dylan would have envied. We were safely through and breaking down the door to the girls' dorm in less than a minute. Stanley waited outside while I raced in to wake Ketty. She was stirring, woken by the noise from the door lock smashing. Several of the other girls looked round, but lay back when they saw me. I understood this attempt to stay out of the trouble we would undoubtedly be in if we were caught.

Ketty's eyes widened as she registered my presence. Her dark, curly hair was a tangled mess around her head but she still managed to look fresh and pretty in the shaft of early sunlight that fell across her bed.

'Ed?' she whispered. 'What the hell are you doing?'

I leaned over the bed. 'We're getting out of here. Now. Hurry. I found this man in San Juan who's helping us. He's got a helicopter and—'

'*What?*' Ketty rubbed her eyes. 'Slow down, Ed, I don't under—'

'There isn't time to explain,' I tugged at her arm. 'The helicopter's waiting – just outside camp.'

At last, Ketty registered what I was saying.

'Are you sure we can trust this man ...?'

'Yes,' I said. 'Absolutely. He's been brilliant.'

'But Geri'll be phoning again in a few days. Why don't we just wait for her? This is all a bit dramatic.' Ketty frowned.

'Because Fernandez will be back long before Geri gets here and I don't want to think about how he'll punish me and Dylan for running off.'

'Okay.' Ketty relented, and reached for the jeans in her locker, neatly folded as per camp rules, then dragged them on over her pyjamas. She grabbed a pair of trainers, then picked up a little troll doll I'd seen her with before – presumably something Nico had given her – and shoved it in her pocket.

She faced me, her mouth set in that determined line I knew so well. 'I'm ready, what about Nico?'

We left the dorm without a backward glance. All the other girls were either asleep or pretending to be. Part of me felt bad leaving them, but – I now realised – compared to Escondite, the camp wasn't so terrible. You might have to work hard and the discipline was harsh, but at least there was plenty of food and hot water and you knew, in the end, you'd get to go home.

I led Ketty outside the dorm to where Stanley was waiting. He nodded a greeting, then spoke soft and fast.

'I can hear noises from the end of the corridor. Ed, get your Lockdown at the ready.'

I could feel Ketty's astonished eyes on me as we crept along the corridor. I wondered what she thought of this new version of me ...

Ed O'Brien. Man of action. Despite my sweaty palms and thumping heart, I liked how it made me feel. My dad would too. He was always saying I wasn't tough enough.

I almost laughed, imagining his face if he could see me now: all stealth and focus, weaponed-up and primed for action.

Ahead of us, round a bend in the corridor, a door creaked open. We could hear anxious, whispered voices.

'The window's broken. Someone's inside.' That was Don.

'Not Nico *again*,' Cindy said.

'I don't think so, he's never broken a window before.'

Their footsteps along the corridor were getting nearer. I stopped just before the bend in the corridor. If we waited here we could catch them as they rounded the corner.

I looked round at Stanley to check I had his approval. He nodded and stepped back against the wall. Ketty stopped too. She looked at me anxiously, but I didn't have time to reassure her. All my attention was on the footsteps coming towards us along the corridor round the bend.

Don was speaking again. 'We need to phone Fernandez.'

Stanley, Ketty and I flattened ourselves against the wall

'Awesome,' Cindy drawled sarcastically. 'Fernandez'll be ecstatic when he hears that—'

Wham.

As Don and Cindy rounded the corner, Stanley and I leaped forward, Lockdowns outstretched. I thrust mine at Cindy.

Ratchet. Sparks. Thud.

She fell to the floor. Ketty shrieked. Don lay beside her, similarly dispatched by Stanley.

'Come on.' Stanley raced off to the main door and slid the bolts. As we followed him through, Ketty whispered anxiously: 'Who *is* he? Why's he helping us?'

128

'I'll explain later,' I said.

Stanley looked over at the building where Nico and the other boys were sleeping.

'I'll get Nico,' he said. 'You take Ketty to the helicopter. Tell Goldie to get the engine running.'

13: REVELATION

I raced off, Ketty at my side. She was still asking questions about Stanley. I answered as best I could, but I was all pumped up with the adrenalin of the situation and it was hard to formulate proper explanations of everything that had happened during the night.

We reached the helicopter. Dylan was awake now and leaning against the body of the machine. She raised her eyebrows as we raced up.

'Nice work, Chino Boy,' she said. 'Where's Nico?'

'Stanley's bringing him.'

'How did you meet this man?' Ketty asked Dylan, clearly hoping for a more coherent reply from her than she'd been getting from me.

Dylan shrugged. 'He's not my find,' she said. 'I got chloroformed and taken to some hellhole earlier. Ed turned up with Stanley. They got me out, though they didn't manage it without *knocking* me out.' She looked at me suspiciously. 'Did *you* attack me with that stun gun? Your girlfriend over there wouldn't say.'

I shrugged, as Luz appeared from the other side of the helicopter. Her eyes widened with relief as she saw me.

'Eds,' she ran towards me, 'estais okay?' She flung her arms around me and hugged me tightly.

I glanced at Dylan and Ketty. Dylan's eyebrows were raised so high they were practically in her hairline. Ketty was frowning.

'Who the hell's this?' she said.

I met her eyes, unable to resist. Was that *jealousy* I was hearing?

This is Luz, I thought-spoke. *She was being held prisoner with Dylan. I had to help her.*

Right. Inside Ketty's mind I sensed confusion and concern and a slight sense of invaded territory.

But nothing you could seriously call jealousy.

I sighed, distracted for a second by how Ketty's mind felt. Everyone's heads are different, you see. I mean, obviously people's moods change all the time, but most people have their own signature 'feel' as well. With Nico it was the intensity that underpinned everything, with the man in the Madelina, that overlay of rage. Ketty's mind had a base of steely determination – like a rock over which a series of fluctuating moods flowed like tides.

I tried to focus. I could sense Ketty trying to control her own thoughts – to conceal some of the anxiety she was feeling.

It's going to be OK, Ketts, I thought-spoke. *We're safe now.*

'Eds, quien es ella?' Luz's anxious voice beside me brought me back to the present.

I broke the connection with Ketty and looked down at Luz, making eye contact immediately.

Quien es ella? Who is she? Inside Luz's head, the question was even more vehement. The baseline of calm was still there, but another emotion – definitely jealousy this time, I thought – pricked at its edges.

Mi amiga, I thought-spoke back, quickly. *Solamente mi amiga. Just my friend.*

Okay. I could feel the smile in Luz's mind spreading out, easing her thoughts.

'Hey, lover boy.' This time it was Dylan's voice that jerked me back to reality. 'Don't you think we should get inside the helicopter? This Stanley guy's running towards us with Nico – and Nico doesn't look conscious – we could be in trouble.'

I jerked away from Luz and turned to Goldie, remembering Stanley's instruction.

'Stanley wanted you to start the engine,' I said. Goldie leaped into the pilot's seat. Seconds later, the engine roared into life.

Stanley was only a few metres away now, Nico slung over his shoulder. He ran up, panting, and deposited Nico in the back of the helicopter.

'He thought I was attacking him … threw a damn locker at me.' He frowned. 'Though I don't know how he managed to reach the locker – or lift it – that fast.'

I glanced at the others. Nico had obviously used his tele-kinesis as self-defence.

'Is he all right?' Ketty asked.

'He'll be fine,' Stanley said. 'I had to knock him out other-wise we'd have been there too long. Sorry, Ed, I should have taken you with me to explain.'

I couldn't help but feel a little puffed up by pride at this apology. The three girls were all looking at me like I was some kind of hero.

We all got into the helicopter. I noticed that Luz pushed her way past Ketty to the seat beside me. Ketty gave an annoyed sniff.

'Everyone on board?' Stanley grinned, yelling above the noise of the engine and the whirr of the blades.

I couldn't help but grin back. Everyone was safe. We were escaping from the Camp and, best of all, I had girls prac-tically fighting over me. And Luz was definitely interested. Beautiful, special Luz.

I couldn't believe my luck. As Stanley slammed the door shut and got in up front, I glanced over my shoulder at Nico. He was moaning softly, his eyes still shut.

Eat your heart out, Nico, I thought to myself. *I'm the one seeing all the action now.*

Feeling ridiculously cheerful, I put my arm round Luz and we took off.

Of course, once we were airborne, I felt sick again. But even that couldn't stop me feeling pretty pleased with myself.

133

Stanley turned round and shouted over the noise of the helicopter that we'd be travelling direct to a heliport just outside Madrid.

'You'll be able to contact whoever you want there,' he yelled.

Ketty turned to pass the news on to Dylan, who immediately leaned forward and grabbed my shoulder through the seats.

'Who *is* this guy?' she asked, pointing at Stanley.

'Yeah,' Ketty echoed. 'You haven't explained why he's helping us or how you met him or anything.'

'He's an ex-soldier passing through on business. He saw me at the Madelina – the bar in San Juan. It's just coincidence he found me.' I swallowed, fighting back the nausea that swelled in my guts now we were airborne. 'He's sound. Honest.'

I sat back, too sick to speak any more. Clearly neither Ketty nor Dylan were really satisfied with my answer, but they were just going to have to wait till we landed for a more detailed explanation of how Stanley had found and helped me.

The sun was high in the sky by the time we landed. I stumbled out of the helicopter with relief. We were in what looked like a private heliport. Just a few other machines on the ground and a handful of men wandering around – some in overalls, others looking more like office workers in suits and smart shirts. Stanley seemed to know everyone. In fact, I got the impression that the people at the heliport were a little bit afraid of him. They were certainly very deferential, swarming round as we landed, offering help with anything and everything.

I figured maybe Stanley's company – and his position within it – was more important than he'd let on.

Stanley certainly seemed quite used to the attention. He ordered us to be taken into a nearby prefab office building. It wasn't quite so blisteringly hot here as it had been in the desert, but the sun still beat down on our heads with a fierce glare. I was glad to get inside.

'Can we make a call from here?' I asked.

'Soon.' Stanley sounded distracted. 'I just have some stuff to deal with.' He led us into a small, windowless room in the prefab hut. A sofa stood in one corner, a table and chairs in another. An air-con unit blasted away noisily, and rather ineffectually, high on the walls above our heads.

One of the men in overalls deposited Nico on the sofa, then left. Immediately Nico groaned and raised his hand to his head. He'd drifted into a sound sleep on the flight, like Dylan had done earlier.

Stanley glanced over as Nico's eyelids flickered.

'Back in a moment,' he said.

As the door shut behind him, everyone started talking at me.

'Que pasa, Eds?' Luz asking, clutching my arm.

'Yeah, Chino Boy, what's he doing leaving us in here?' Dylan said.

'Why hasn't he given us a phone?' Ketty said.

'It's fine,' I said, trying to speak to everyone at once. 'He's just busy. He'll sort us out in—'

135

'No … no …' Nico was staggering to his feet, leaning heavily on the sofa behind him.

Everyone turned and stared at him. His brown eyes had a glassy, unwell look to them, but there was no mistaking the fear in his expression.

'Where are we? Where is he?' Nico lurched forwards, stumbling against Ketty.

She held his arm, her face terrified.

'Nico, what's the matter?'

She glanced at me. I shook my head.

'We have to get out of here. Door … Ed … door …' Nico gasped.

I turned to the door behind me.

'Open it …' Nico looked completely panic-stricken.

'Calm down,' I said, talking almost as much to myself as to him. 'There's nothing wrong.'

Dylan let out an exasperated sigh. 'Just open it, Ed.' She darted behind me and rattled the door handle. It didn't open.

We all stared at it. A cold, sick feeling lodged itself in my stomach.

'We're locked in,' Ketty said in disbelief.

'Eds?' Luz gripped my arm. Her fingers were trembling.

My head spun. The cold, sick feeling had reached my throat now. I looked over at Nico, trying to meet his eyes, but he was still staring, horrified at the locked door. He turned and focused on one of the chairs at the table. It rose into the air, teetered for a moment, then fell back to the ground.

Beside me, Luz gasped.

'I just need a few minutes ...' Nico flopped onto the sofa, his head in his hands.

Dylan and Ketty exchanged anxious glances. Ketty sat down beside Nico and put her hand on his back.

'Nico?' she said uncertainly. 'What's going on?'

For a few moments, there was a terrible silence. And then Nico looked up.

'Where's the man who knocked me out at the camp?' he said. 'He got me with a stun gun ... must have got Tommy and Mat and Mig too ...'

I relaxed. *Of course.* This was all just a misunderstanding. Nico had thought Stanley was attacking him earlier, no wonder he was urging us to get away now.

'Outside,' I said. 'But you've got this wrong. His name's Andrew Stanley. He's been brilliant, helping us escape from Fernandez. He even used his helicopter to help rescue you from the camp.'

'Then why's the door locked?' Nico said.

'I don't know,' I admitted, 'but I do know that Stanley's an amazing hero – one of the good guys.'

'No, he's not,' Nico said, fury clouding his dark eyes. 'He's one of the worst.'

'What do you mean?' Dylan asked, putting her hands on her hips. 'Do you *know* him?'

'Yes,' Nico said, 'and so do you. He's the man who was prepared to have Ketty killed – who tried to buy us as weapons – back in Cornwall.'

The cold, sick feeling slammed back, filling my head.

'It *can't* be him,' Ketty breathed, her face blanching.

Dylan's eyes widened. 'No freakin' *way*.'

I stared at Nico. *It wasn't possible, was it?*

'Yeah, well done, Ed.' Nico stood, his eyes and voice savage with contempt. 'Your amazing hero is only frigging Blake Carson.'

14: ALONE

I couldn't bear it. I had brought us all to Blake Carson, a violent weapons dealer and one of the most dangerous criminals in the country.

I told Nico, Ketty and Dylan the whole story of how I'd met him. Even as I was explaining the series of coincidences that had led to us sitting here in this prefab hut I realised just how gullible I'd been.

Nico was furious. 'Didn't it all seem a bit convenient?' he roared. 'You're running away and he *happens* to be on the same street ... then *happens* to have the weapons you need to rescue Dylan and me and Ketty?'

'He said he was a sales and marketing director with an electronics security firm,' I stammered. 'So I thought the Lockdowns made sense.'

'Well, we all thought *you* made sense, but in fact you're a tool and a total freakin' liability,' Dylan snapped from across the room.

Nico rolled his eyes. I couldn't bear to look at Ketty.

Luz was still clinging to my arm. I was pretty sure she didn't understand what we were saying, though she could see clearly enough that everyone was furious with me.

My heart sank. Once she knew how I'd let everyone down, she'd be as pissed off with me as everyone else.

'And what about *why* he was prepared to help you?' Nico stormed on. 'Didn't it occur to you to be the slightest bit suspicious that a complete stranger was prepared to mount three separate rescue operations, all of which put *him* at risk *and* involved using his so-called *company* helicopter?'

'There was no signal – we couldn't phone anyone . . . there was no one else who *could* help . . .'

'Did you *see* there was no signal?' Nico raged. 'Or did Carson just tell you? 'And what about landlines?'

I looked down. I hadn't ever seen how many bars were on Carson's mobile phone. I'd taken the whole thing on trust.

'He said a truck had driven into the local power lines and that *nothing* was working.' As I spoke the whole thing sounded ridiculous. How could I have fallen for it?

'You're a frigging idiot,' Nico went on. 'Even if all that were true, didn't you ask yourself *why* would some random bloke off the street go to all these lengths to help?'

'He said he and his wife couldn't have children . . . that they felt they should help kids when they could.' I bit my lip, remembering how it had felt like a good omen when Stanley told me his wife's name – Sandra – the same as my stepmum's. That must have been made up too, I realised, like his whole background story.

'But not *all* kids,' Dylan pointed out. 'He left the younger ones from the Escondite behind – and everyone else in the camp.'

'He took Luz.' I looked across the room.

'Only because you insisted,' Dylan said.

'Well, *you* came with him,' I said to Dylan.

'Don't try and pin this on me.' Dylan's voice rose. 'I was *unconscious* until we were in the helicopter.'

'Basically, Carson sold you some ridiculous sob story,' Nico said, more quietly, 'and you fell for it like a complete prat.'

Ketty laid a hand on Nico's arm. 'I think Ed feels bad enough,' she said. 'We all thought Carson was in prison, remember?'

I shot her a grateful glance, my face burning.

There was an awkward silence. Ketty cleared her throat. 'The important thing now is that we work together to try and get out of here, yes?'

'What a good idea,' Dylan drawled nastily. 'Had any visions lately that'll help us do that? Or are you still running on empty?'

'Shut up, Dylan,' Nico said.

'What is visions?' Luz said, faintly.

Ketty looked away.

'No, go on, Ketty,' Dylan sneered. 'Tell us how exactly you're planning on getting us to "work together" so we can get out of here.'

'Don't speak to her like that!' I snapped.

141

'Back off, Ed.' Nico sprang to his feet, fists clenched. 'Don't start frigging defending Ketty in front of me or I'll frigging punch you, you frigging *idiot*. It's your fault we're all here.' He took a furious step towards me.

'Nico,' Ketty said, crossly, 'this isn't going to—'

'Well, I see the cat's out of the bag vis-à-vis my true identity, then,' Blake Carson said from the doorway.

I spun round. We'd been so wrapped up in our argument, we hadn't even heard him unlock the door. He was standing there, half-smiling, all tall and mean-looking.

The cold sick feeling I'd had before settled like a stone in my guts.

It didn't matter how I tried to justify it. Nico was right, I *had* been an idiot. A *total* idiot. I should have sensed something was wrong.

Nico immediately raised his hand. The chair he'd struggled to lift telekinetically before now soared into the air.

Luz gasped as the chair flew towards Carson.

And then Carson raised his hand and fired the gun at Nico. The chair fell to the floor.

Nico staggered back and slumped into the sofa. His eyes closed.

'Nooo!' Ketty screamed. She flung herself down beside him. 'Nico!'

'You've killed him!' Dylan shrieked.

'Don't be ridiculous,' Carson snarled.

I stared at Nico's arm. A tiny dart was sticking out, just above Nico's elbow. There was no blood. I turned and stared at the gun Carson had used. It was some kind of tranquilliser.

'What did you shoot him with?' I said, my voice surprisingly steady, considering the anger and fear coursing through me.

'A non-barbiturate sedative. Just enough to keep him quiet while I explain the deal to the rest of you.'

I froze. 'We had a deal yesterday,' I said angrily. 'You were going to help me and my friends get away from Fernandez.'

Carson laughed. 'And I did, Ed, remember? Now we're just moving on to phase two . . .'

My face burned. I'd been such a fool. And now Nico and Dylan were furious with me – and Ketty and Luz would never look at me with admiration in their eyes again. So much for Ed O'Brien, Man of Action.

I should never have even believed changing was possible. I was useless, like my dad said.

I always had been and I always would be.

I looked up.

Everyone else was still staring at Carson.

'So go on, then.' Dylan crossed her arms and shook back her hair. 'What's the deal?'

Carson narrowed his eyes. 'The four of you are going to make me a lot of money.' He turned and signalled to two men waiting outside. As they walked in and hoisted Nico up off the sofa, Ketty spoke, her voice low and bitter.

'*How* are we going to make you money?' she said.

'As I'm sure you've already been told, I trade in biological weapons,' Carson said smoothly. 'You, kiddos, are the ultimate biological weapons. All I have to do now is find a buyer.'

'*What?*' Dylan said.

'What about Luz?' I said. 'What are you going to do with her?'

The atmosphere in the room tightened. The two men carrying Nico left the room. For a second I hoped that Carson would fix his eyes on me. In my fantasy scenario I would be able to hold him with my mind-reading while the others escaped … Except what about all the guards? And where would we go? And how would we rescue Nico?

Carson fixed his gaze on a spot to the left of my nose. 'We'll have to see about Luz.'

I shivered at the sinister tone in his voice. What the hell did *that* mean?

And then Carson raised his tranquilliser gun and pointed it at me. 'For now, Ed, I suggest you stick to worrying about yourself.'

As he squeezed the trigger I could hear Ketty start to shriek. A sharp pain in my upper arm. And then the room faded to black.

15: ON THE BOAT

Bump. Bump. Something pointy and hard in my back. Head pounding, I struggled to open my eyes. My eyelids felt stuck together. With a huge effort I forced them open. Darkness.

Panic leaped into my throat. Why couldn't I see? Was I blind? Suddenly I was wide awake. For a few moments thoughts careered wildly around my head. Had Carson blinded me to stop me mind-reading people? I gasped in a breath, registering for the first time that I was squashed and sitting on a hard floor that somehow seemed to be moving and the pointy thing in my back was either a blunt knife or a bony elbow.

'Hello?' My voice quavered in the darkness.

'Ed?' Ketty's voice came from close by, to my left.

I reached out my hand, groping into the black. I touched an arm. It was warm against my hand. The pointy thing moved. Ketty's elbow.

'Ketty?' I tried to shuffle forward, but there was no room. 'Where are we?'

As I asked the question the movement of the floor beneath – a soft swelling motion – gave me the answer. We were at sea.

'We're locked in a cage in a lorry,' Ketty said. 'And the lorry's on a boat.'

I sat, trying to get my head round this information. 'Where are we going?'

'I don't know.' Ketty's voice shook. 'After Carson shot you with that tranquilliser Dylan went a bit mad and he shot her too, then he looked at me and Luz and asked if he needed to shoot us too or whether we'd behave and I couldn't see any point in *all* of us being knocked out so I said fine and he blindfolded us and we got back in the helicopter and flew to the sea. I could smell it and hear it. Then he split us up and put you and me in this cage in a lorry. I guess the others must be in another one.' She sniffed. 'I've just been waiting for you to wake up. Hoping you were OK.' Her voice cracked.

I felt down her arm and squeezed her hand.

'I'm so sorry about Carson, Ketts,' I said, my own voice cracking now. 'I didn't—'

'Don't.' She squeezed my hand back. 'You were only trying to do the right thing. Nico and Dylan know that. They're just scared.'

I nodded, then realised that she couldn't see me in the pitch black. 'Er . . . I guess.'

'What d'you think Carson is going to do with us?' Ketty went on, as the boat pitched and rolled underneath us. 'What was all that stuff about biological weapons?'

146

'I don't know.' I hesitated. 'Have you had any visions since we left camp?'

'Not a flicker.' Ketty sighed. 'I keep trying but nothing happens.'

I hesitated again. 'I've been trying to work on my telepathy,' I said.

Silence.

'*Work* on it?' Ketty said. 'That's not like you.'

'I know.' I rubbed my forehead.

'So what have you been working *on* exactly?' Ketty said.

'Well, you know that thing I do where if I look into someone's eyes I have to mind-read them?' I said.

'Yes.' I could tell from the sound of Ketty's voice that she'd turned slightly and was facing me.

'I was wondering if it *had* to be like that,' I said, thinking about my failed attempts at remote telepathy. 'If maybe I could do it a different way.'

'Yeah, I've wondered about that too,' Ketty said. She shifted again. I could just imagine her sitting up straighter and tucking her hair behind her ears in that determined way of hers. 'I mean, it doesn't really make sense ... why should you get sucked in just because you look directly at someone? I mean, I've wondered if ... whether it's really just some way for you to avoid making eye contact.'

In the darkness, I froze. What was she saying? 'But—'

'I don't mean you do it on purpose,' Ketty hurried on, 'just that making sure you don't look people in the eye has become a habit you've got into which you've convinced yourself

147

you *have* to do, but which is actually just a convenient way of not ... not ... really *connecting* with people' She paused and the dark space between us filled up with the silence. 'I thought that's what you meant when you said you were trying to do your telepathy a different way. Wasn't it?'

I sat, rigid in the blackness, Ketty's words going round my head. Was what she said true? Was mind-reading on eye contact actually something I could choose *not* to do?

'Ed?' Ketty's hand brushed my shoulder. 'Ed? I'm sorry, I didn't mean to upset you.'

I took a deep breath. 'You didn't,' I said. 'You just made me think.'

'About?'

'I've been trying to mind-read at a distance since we got to camp. You know, get in touch with my mum and dad at home somehow.'

'Really?' Ketty's voice burned with excitement. 'That's a brilliant idea.'

'Yeah.' I sighed. 'Except it hasn't worked. I thought it was because I needed the eye contact but if you're right and I don't, then there's no reason why I shouldn't be able to work out what *anyone's* thinking.'

'Try me now,' Ketty said. 'Go on ... what colour am I thinking of?'

'Okay.' I sat for second. How to start? I took a few deep breaths and focused my attention on my mental image of Ketty's face. In my mind's eye I saw her clearly – the golden-brown eyes, wide and eager, the snub nose and the curve

148

of her cheek, all framed by her dark curly hair. 'I'm seeing you,' I said. 'But only on the outside.'

'Keep going,' she said. 'Don't force it.'

I tried to relax. It wasn't easy being all cramped up in this cage. Another deep breath. I let my body release, sinking down into the ground. Beneath me, the gentle movement of the sea was rhythmic and soothing. More deep breaths. I kept Ketty's face in my mind as I imagined looking into her dark eyes. *There she was. There.*

With a whoosh, I was transported. But where? Was I actually inside Ketty's head? My focus flickered on and off, like a dying light bulb. I sensed a backdrop of stubborn determination ... a focus on a word ... a colour ...

Yellow? I thought-spoke.

Ed? As Ketty thought-spoke back, the connection slid away.

I frowned, trying to bring it back, but it was no good.

'Hey, you did it,' Ketty exclaimed.

'Yeah, for about two seconds,' I said with a sigh.

'Never mind, that was an *amazing* start,' Ketty said, her voice filled with awe.

I grinned. She was right, it *was* a start. Something to build on, at least.

'Can you try and reach Nico now?' Ketty said, all excited.

Nico. As she said his name, my sense of triumph evaporated. It didn't matter how powerful I became at reading people's minds, Ketty's first thought would always be for *him.*

149

'Sure,' I said, trying to hide the hurt in my voice. I brought Nico's face to mind – the dark eyes, full of mischief, the high cheekbones and smooth skin … it struck me as I focused on a mental picture of his face, that I'd never seen Nico with so much as a single spot. How unfair was that?

I slowed my breathing, as I had before, and concentrated on Nico's face in my mind's eye. It was harder to imagine looking into his eyes. Maybe because I'd done it less. Or maybe because, after the scornful way he'd spoken to me earlier, the inside of Nico's head was the last place I wanted to be.

I kept going but it didn't feel right. I was exhausted, I realised, from connecting with Ketty and forcing this attempt to reach Nico. After a couple of minutes I gave up.

'It's not working,' I said. 'I'll try again in a minute.'

'Okay.' Ketty sounded disappointed. 'At least you know it's poss—'

A banging sound, metal on metal, broke across her words. Light flooded the van, blinding me. Heavy footsteps pounded across the inside of the van.

I blinked, my eyes adjusting to the light. One of Carson's men was standing over us, peering in through the bars of the cage. He raised his hand. Another tranquilliser gun.

I opened my mouth to say 'No', but before I could speak I felt the prick of the dart in my arm and was out cold.

Sometime later I awoke, my head pounding, my mouth dry. It took a few moments for me to remember everything that had happened. As I did, my eyes sprang open. I was in a bare, sunlit room. Light poured in through the only window, high overhead. A single light bulb hung from the centre of the room. Nothing on the walls. No furniture.

It was a cell.

Stomach twisting with fear, I eased myself off the low camp bed I'd been placed on. My right arm was numb from the way I'd lain on it. I rubbed it, swallowing to create some moisture in my mouth. I had never felt so thirsty in my life.

Where was everyone else?

I was about to stand up when the door opened. Carson walked in, carrying a chair.

'Good, you're awake,' he said.

I glanced up at the window and the bright sunlight. The room was swelteringly hot – an even fiercer, drier heat than the desert in Spain.

'Where am I?' I said.

'North Africa.' Carson waved his hand as if to suggest the detail of our exact location wasn't important. 'And, before you ask, your friends are safe . . . all of them. Would you like some water?'

I nodded, rubbing my forehead. My neck was stiff and sore and my brain felt like it was operating through a fog, but I had to pull myself together. I had to find out what Carson was planning to do with us.

As I was thinking all this, Carson rose from his chair and disappeared outside. A second later he was back, a full litre bottle of water in his hand. He passed it to me and I took a couple of huge gulps.

'Careful.' His thin lips twisted into a smile. 'You'll make yourself sick drinking that fast.'

I shrugged.

Carson put on a pair of mirrored sunglasses. 'These are just a precaution, kiddo.' He tapped his temple. 'Access denied and all that.'

My heart beat faster as I remembered how I'd managed that brief connection with Ketty – and without eye contact – earlier. Maybe I should try and get inside Carson's head now?

No. Better to wait until my own head was clearer … until he wasn't sitting right in front of me …

'I expect you're wondering what I'm going to do with you.' Carson leaned back in his chair.

'Actually, I was wondering how long I'd been unconscious,' I said. 'And why you're not still in prison.'

Carson sat up. 'It's been about twelve hours since the injection in the boat. Twenty-four or so since the first tranquilliser in Spain.'

My mouth fell open. I'd lost a whole *day*? I took another sip of water.

'As for prison,' Carson went on, 'all the charges against me were dropped. I'd have thought Geri Paterson would have told you that.'

I looked away. Geri had a habit of not telling us important things. I couldn't imagine why she hadn't let us know Carson was on the loose, but at least it explained why she was so keen to fake our deaths and create new identities for us.

'I've been looking for you since I was released,' Carson

went on. 'And I have to say I was getting nowhere fast until I picked up some blog about a kid in a bar in San Juan who did a mean mind-reading trick.'

I shook my head, inwardly cursing Jorge's greed. 'So what *are* you going to do with me ... with us?' I said.

'Glad you asked, kiddo.' Carson stood up. 'I've got a job for you – and you'd better not let me down.'

16: THE INTERROGATION

I stared up at Carson, my head still throbbing.

'You've got a job for me?' I said. 'Doing what?'

Carson crossed his arms and leaned against the wall. 'There's a man next door who has resisted all my attempts to get him to tell me a piece of information that I badly need,' he said. 'You, kiddo, are my passport to that information. And before you even think about saying "no", I suggest you remember which one of us has the gun.' He smiled and patted his jacket, outlining the holster underneath.

I stood up, feeling shaky on my legs. I'd have to go along with this for now – there was no choice. I stumbled after Carson into a concrete corridor. Other doors led off down both sides. I just had time to wonder if the others were locked in any of those rooms, before Carson was pushing me into another bleak, concrete cell. This one had no windows and was even more stifling than the room I'd been kept in. A mirror ran the length of one wall and a single rickety table stood in the middle of the room, a chair on either side.

'Sit,' Carson ordered.

I sat down in one of the chairs, my heart beating fast. Carson was clearly going to make me mind-read someone. But who? And why?

The door opened again and two black men walked in. The first was dressed in a torn, bloodstained shirt. He limped to the chair on the opposite side of the table from me then stood, head bowed. The other man, smartly dressed in a crisp cotton suit, with large, damp sweat patches under the arms, prodded him into the chair, then stood back. A gun rested inside the holster strapped to his belt.

The first man looked up. I gasped. His face was swollen and bruised – one eye almost completely obscured behind a blood-encrusted gash. He frowned, the glassy expression on his face coming momentarily into focus as he registered I was sitting in front of him. He hung his head again and I turned to Carson, feeling sick.

'This man knows the location of some property that was stolen from a friend of mine,' he said, speaking before I had a chance to say anything. 'I want you to find out where that property is. Go on, mind-read him – his name is Charles Tsonga.'

At the mention of his name, Tsonga looked up. I glanced past him, to the mirror at the end of the room. I could see the whole scene reflected in front of me – the back of Tsonga's head, where another sizable gash made a dark red line across his closely-shaved scalp, the rickety table, the guard standing impassively to one side, Carson, tall and thin in his mirrored

155

shades, leaning over me, and, in the middle of the scene, me – all anxious eyes and tousled hair. I stared at myself in the mirror and remembered the remote telepathy I'd managed yesterday.

If I could do that, then maybe I didn't need to do this. Confidence surged through me. Maybe I could look straight into Tsonga's eyes and *not* mind-read him.

'Ed.' Carson's voice sounded a warning note. 'Get on with it.'

Tsonga was staring defiantly, at me. I took a deep breath and looked up, into his bloodshot brown eyes. I held his gaze, feeling and fighting the impulse to dive into his mind. It actually wasn't that hard, I realised with a jolt. All that time I'd believed I had no choice but to mind-read on eye contact. *God*, maybe Ketty had been right and it had all been one great big unconscious excuse to justify my own shyness.

'Ed?' Carson said, a trace of impatience in his voice. 'What can you see?'

I hesitated a second. 'Nothing,' I said. 'It's not working.'

Carson's hand thumped down on the table. Both Tsonga and I jumped. The guard stepped smartly forward, yanking the gun out of his holster. He held it straight out in front of him, pointing from me, to Tsonga, then back to me.

I sucked in my breath, fighting a sudden, panicky urge to pee. Carson held up his hand and the guard stepped back.

'Okay, Ed, let's try again,' he said softly.

I took a gulp from the water bottle that was still in my hand. Tsonga's eyes fixed on the clear liquid. His thirst was

156

unmistakable. I glanced at Carson for permission to share the drink. He nodded.

I held the bottle out and Tsonga took it.

'Thank you.' His heavily-accented voice cracked as he spoke.

'You're welcome,' I said.

Tsonga took a couple of large gulps, then put the bottle down on the table between us. 'I will not speak,' he said.

'Ed, go on,' Carson prompted.

'But it's not working,' I said, as emphatically as I could.

'I don't believe you.' Carson's voice was laced with menace. I could feel the tip of a gun against the back of my head. 'Hurry up, or I'll send this guard to shoot your friends. One by one, until you do what I say.'

Tsonga was staring at us; his eyes looked clearer now he'd drunk some water, but his forehead was creased with a frown.

I swallowed. There was no choice.

'Now, Ed,' Carson said.

I looked into Tsonga's eyes. This time I let the old impulse to dive in take over. With a whoosh, I was there, inside his mind – an angry, scared place, a low, steady energy underneath.

Instinctively I knew Tsonga was a good man. Whatever he was hiding from Carson, he was hiding it for a good reason.

And I was about to expose his secret.

Hi, I thought-spoke.

What? Who? How? Tsonga's thought-speech exploded in panic-stricken fury.

157

I held back, like I always do when I'm inside someone's mind for the first time. It seems to help to give people a little time to adjust to me. I counted to ten, waiting, but fragments of Tsonga's thoughts and feelings were still whirling round his head. Maybe he was too stressed by being held and beaten to be able to settle at all.

'Find out where the weapons are held,' Carson hissed in my ear.

I'm not going to hurt you, I thought-spoke, trying to calm Tsonga down. *Carson just wants information. Where are the weapons?*

No ... no ... no ... Another explosion of terrified fury. *Please, no. Do not ask this. I cannot tell you.*

I broke the connection and turned to Carson.

'Well?'

'He can't tell me,' I said. 'He doesn't know.'

Carson swore. In a swift move he grabbed my shirt under the neck and bunched it in a fist that pressed into my chin. 'Enough pissing about,' he said. 'I know what you can do. Get inside his head and find out where the weapons are. Which village. Which house. How well protected ...' He shoved me away and pressed his gun against my head again. There was a loud click as he cocked it.

Heart pounding so loudly it seemed to echo round the tiny room, I turned back to Tsonga. He was staring down at the table, rocking back and forth.

Carson signalled to the guard, who came over and forced Tsonga's head up. I met his eyes.

158

Please, please, please ... the earlier fury was now mostly fear.

I'm sorry but you have to tell me where the weapons are.

I can't, you don't understand. My brother is hiding them. And if they find him, they will kill him – and his family and my ... my little girl. We need these weapons to fight back against Djounsou's army. Please, please help me.

I badly wanted to break the connection, to refuse Carson. It was evil, forcing this man to reveal information that would hurt his family. And whoever this Djounsou was, I was certain that he needed fighting against. I felt sick to my stomach, yet what could I do? Ketty, Dylan, Nico and Luz's lives were in danger if I *didn't* do it.

'Find the information I need, Ed,' Carson hissed in my ear, clearly sensing my thoughts, 'or your friends die ... one by one.'

I steeled myself, focusing fully on Tsonga.

I'm sorry, I thought-spoke.

Please, think of my daughter, Victoria. She is only five. Please, I beg you.

I'm sorry. I dived into Tsonga's mind. After my experience reading minds in the Spanish bar, I had learned to hold less tightly to the concrete thoughts I came across and to let my instinct guide me – to try less, in a way, while remaining completely focused. In moments I'd probed deeper into his thoughts and feelings.

My sense that he was a good person was only reinforced. I saw great loss – his wife and their second child had died in childbirth. There was also anger at Carson and his bullying and – far more powerful – fury at the man he'd mentioned before, Djounsou. Plus exhaustion ... and physical pain ... and a strong religious faith.

Where are the weapons? I thought-spoke, keeping my communication as calm as possible. I could feel Tsonga's panic rising.

No, no, no. <u>Mahore.</u> No. <u>My brother.</u> No ... <u>Church, St Luke's, cellar.</u> No, no, no ...

I sighed. It was always the same. As soon as people knew what you wanted, what they *mustn't* think about, that was always the very thing that thrust itself to the front of their minds. But I didn't need to tell Carson the whole story. If I told him the overall place, but gave a different specific location for the weapons, Tsonga's brother might have time to see Carson's men coming and get to safety.

'Mahore,' I said out loud.

Noooo. Inside Tsonga's head something had broken. Like glass that had cracked and shattered. *I am betraying them, oh God, please help me.*

It's okay, I tried to reassure him, *I won't say where the weapons are or who's responsible.*

You don't understand.

'How well are the guns protected?' Carson asked, his voice tight with excitement. 'Where are they hidden?'

What shall I say? I thought-spoke.

I waited while Tsonga gathered himself.

Tell him the guns are hidden in a hut on the road out of

160

town going west. The hut is on the outskirts of town – it has a . . . a blue painted wall and a red flag on the roof.

I repeated this information.

'How is this hut guarded?' Carson said.

Tell him several men take turns. Usually there are two at the hut at any time.

Again, I repeated the information Tsonga gave me.

'But you should know that they change the location of the hiding place all the time,' I added, pleased with myself for having come up with such a clever way of covering myself, while still protecting Tsonga and his family. 'By the time you reach the hut, the weapons may have been moved.'

I broke the connection.

'Good,' Carson said. 'Good work. You can go now.' He signalled to the guard to take me away.

'You won't hurt him any more?' I asked.

'No, if you've passed on the information you saw correctly, there'll be no need for him to feel more pain.' Carson narrowed his eyes. 'In fact, there'll be no reason for him to feel anything any more.'

17: COMMUNICATION

The guard pushed me out of the room and back into my own. I sank down on the bed, my head in my hands. Did that comment about Tsonga not feeling 'anything any more' mean Carson was planning to kill him?

I looked up, determined to try remote telepathy again. If I'd managed that brief connection with Ketty, then surely if I practised a bit more I'd be able to reach Geri and explain what had happened so she could come here, rescue us *and* save Tsonga and his family. But before I could begin to focus on Geri's face, the guard knocked me out with another injection.

I had no idea what time it was when I finally woke up, but my room was in darkness, though the air was barely less stifling. I was lying on the camp bed, as before. I turned and looked at the door, my head throbbing with every movement. A tiny camera I hadn't noticed before was positioned just above the door, the lens pointing towards the bed. I blinked. Was *that* how Carson had known I was conscious earlier? I quickly closed my eyes again. Even in my fuggy state, I was aware that I had to buy myself enough time to clear my head and attempt to communicate telepathically with Geri.

A few minutes passed. I lay awake, concentrating on keeping my breathing deep and steady. I was desperately thirsty – my mouth felt dry and swollen – and hunger gnawed at my stomach, but I didn't dare look round to see if Carson had left any food or drink in the room. I kept my eyes closed as my head slowly settled and cleared, then started to picture Geri Paterson's face – her piercing birdlike eyes, delicate-featured face and sharply-cut blonde bob. I slowed my breathing and really focused – but nothing happened. I waited, trying not to push it, knowing that half the skill of remote telepathy was in the *not* trying. But still nothing came.

I let out a long sigh. Maybe my head was still too fuzzy. Maybe Geri was simply too far away. Or maybe I didn't have a strong enough emotional connection with her to make a telepathic connection work.

This last thought took me to Ketty ... and to Luz. Would Carson let Luz go? I couldn't imagine he would. And yet what use could he possibly have for a poor Spanish girl from a care home? My stomach twisted as I thought of the terrible danger I'd put her in – a thought which led me back to Tsonga and his fear for his family which led me, inevitably, to my own mum and dad. I'd tried, for the past day or two, not to think about them at all, but now it was as if all the thoughts I'd been pushing away were insisting on rushing back.

163

Almost without acknowledging what I was doing, I focused on Mum's face – her lined forehead and short, greying hair. She's not my real mum, of course, so we don't look anything alike, but I know I've picked up a lot of her expressions. We both share a slightly anxious look behind the eyes, and there's definitely a tightness in the way we smile sometimes.

I concentrated harder, again trying not to push too hard at making the connection.

Nothing.

Misery welled up from my guts. I squeezed my eyes tight shut. *Keep trying*, I said to myself. I moved on to Dad, focusing on his sandy hair, ruddy face and blue eyes. Still nothing.

It was dark outside. Even through closed eyes, I could tell that the dim light which had filtered in from the single high window earlier on had now completely disappeared. Fighting the despair that filled me, I thought of my sisters. Amy, with the same blue eyes as our dad, and little Kim, who looked just like her mum.

At first I moved between them, unable to settle, then I fixed on Amy. She was twelve now and, to be honest, I didn't feel I knew her very well any more. When I left home to go to Fox Academy she was all into her new friends at St Michael's – the girls' Catholic grammar school she'd started at last autumn – and we didn't talk that much. As Mum said, Amy only seemed to have three topics of conversation: her friends, her music and how much she hated everything about

164

her new school – from the overstrict teachers to the minging purple uniform.

Still, we'd been close when we were little. And I couldn't think of anyone else to try. So I steadied my breathing again and focused on Amy's face – wide eyes, arched brows and high cheekbones – all framed by her thick, chestnut-coloured hair.

At first nothing happened. I knew I was pushing at the connection ... trying too hard. I sighed, half giving up, just idly thinking about Amy ... the shape of her face ... her eyes ... And then I felt a flicker ... that strange sense I'd had before, with Ketty, that I was fading in and out of someone else's mind.

I let myself go with the sensation, trying to ride it like a wave. With a sudden 'whoosh' I found myself sucked into Amy's head. *Whoa.* This was a far stronger, more solid connection than I'd had during remote telepathy with Ketty.

I sensed Amy feel my presence and start to panic.

Hey, Amy, I thought-spoke. *It's me, Ed.* I stopped, unsure what to say next and overwhelmed by the tornado of emotion rushing round Amy's head. I wasn't certain it was all brought on by my sudden entrance into her brain, either. God, how did she cope with that level of hysteria on a permanent basis?

Ed? Her thought-speech was pitched almost at a shriek. *Oh. My. God. Ohmigod, ohmigod, ohmi—*

Calm down, Amy. Listen, I don't have much time.

But you're there ... here ... how? Mum and Dad said you were in trouble and you'd gone away to some ... I dunno ...

165

it sounded like a prison, though it can't be worse than here.
Mum actually grounded me for my phone running out of
power yesterday—

Amy, listen—

It's so unfair, she's always picking on me and she's been
going on about keeping quiet about you as well, like I'm some
stupid ... oh my God I can't believe it's you, I mean how are
you doing this?

Slow down. In spite of my terrible predicament, I was
almost laughing at Amy's outburst. Her mind overran with
a feverish imagination. Thoughts and feelings sparked out
of nowhere. I caught glimpses of feuds and tears and every
intense emotion imaginable – all simmering just out of plain
view.

But what's going on, Ed, how is this happening?

Ask Mum and Dad about Medusa, they'll explain every-
thing, I thought-spoke, feeling guilty. Mum and Dad had
insisted that the girls shouldn't know about the Medusa
gene – that it was too weird and upsetting for them. Still, what
choice did I have?

Is this ... this mind-reading real? How do I know I'm not
imagining you?

You're not imagining anything. I'm Ed – if you don't
believe me, check my bedroom – you'll find a shoebox in the
wardrobe. If you look right at the bottom, you'll see my old
chess set. Three of the pawns – that's the littlest figures –
are missing. There's no way anyone else knows about that,
okay?

Okay, I'll check, but how are you doing this? How long have you been able to?

A while. It's why I went away to that boarding school.

Is it why you're in trouble now?

Sort of. Look, Amy, I don't have time to explain everything right now. I need you to tell Mum and Dad I've contacted you. I don't know where I am, but it's somewhere in North Africa, and I'm a prisoner ... we all are ...

A prisoner! Who's 'we', for God's sake? Ed, this can't be happening.

It is. Check my chess set. Listen. There are four of us. Mum and Dad know about some of it. You have to tell them to contact Geri Paterson—

Who?

Her name is Geri Paterson. They'll know how to get hold of her. You need to pass on this message – that the four of us are being held prisoner by Blake Carson, somewhere in North Africa, and she has to track him down and get us out. I'll contact you again in a few hours and—

Light flooded the room behind my eyes as the door was flung open. I lost the connection.

Amy was gone.

18: THE PLAN

I looked round, half my head still focused on my telepathic conversation with Amy. Blake Carson was standing by the open door of my room. He watched me as I sat up, then pulled on a pair of dark sunglasses.

'Were you asleep?' he said.

'Er, yes.' I faked a yawn and glanced up at the window. It was still dark outside.

'Good, I need you rested.'

'What for?' My heart skipped a beat.

'Handover.'

'Handover?' I stared blankly at him.

'Come on, Ed. You must have noticed the two-way mirror in the interrogation room next door.'

I thought back to the room and how I'd noticed my reflection and the gash in the back of Tsonga's head. 'Who was watching me?'

'A man called General Djounsou and a couple of his

closest aides. The General is *very* interested in having you help them.'

General Djounsou. I remembered that name from my telepathic communication with Tsonga. He was the man Tsonga and his brother were fighting.

'Help how?' My head reeled with all this new information.

'Djounsou's tired of the endless insurgencies against him. He believes he spends too much time firefighting all the rebellions against him, and not enough building his empire. He sees you as a fast, effective interrogation method. One that will get him fail-safe information to bring the recent spate of uprisings to a swift end.'

'Like telling them who, and where the resistance is happening,' I said. 'Like I did with Tsonga?' A cold sensation washed over me at the thought of how many people this could put in terrible danger.

'Exactly. Plus Djounsou is aware that news of your strange abilities will spread quickly. Most of the villages in this region are full of poor, uneducated people who, underneath their Man U shirts and happy-clappy Christianity, still believe in spirits and magic and all kinds of whacko nonsense. Your mind-reading will *terrify* them. Djounsou knows you're the best propaganda weapon he could have.'

'I can't work for Djounsou,' I said, horrified. 'I can't use my ability to terrorise people.'

'You don't have a choice, Ed,' Carson said, smoothly. 'Quite apart from the consequences to yourself and your

169

family back home if you don't cooperate, we've been experimenting with Cobra, Mamba and Viper too. And the girls will suffer if you don't do what you're told.'

It took me a second to register what he meant – then I remembered . . . the snake names were the codes William Fox had given us when he implanted us with the Medusa gene. Nico was Cobra, Dylan was Mamba and Ketty was Viper. I bit my lip.

'We've discovered that, as I thought, Nico's Gift makes him highly valuable – his telekinesis is a fantastic weapon, as you know. Dylan's ability is far less intrinsically useful.'

'Why?'

'Dylan's ability to see physical harm coming her way and deal with it protects only herself. We've taken loads of blood from her and I've got people researching ways of unlocking her ability from that – to decode it, if you like. So while Dylan's skill is useful, she herself is of very limited value. Likewise Ketty – I've pushed her quite hard and she's been unable to convince me she can see any further than the end of her nose.'

My guts twisted at the thought of Ketty being bullied by Carson. And then I remembered Luz.

'What about the Spanish girl we came with?' I said.

'I have no plans for her.' Carson waved his hand dismissively. 'She's certainly not part of the deal with Djounsou.'

I felt sick. Luz was just fallout from Carson's game, with no value to him. And it was my fault that she was even here.

Carson fell silent. 'Djounsou is waiting to see if you gave him accurate information about the weapons stash in Mahore. If he's impressed, you'll be taken away from here to wherever he's based. If not ... well, I've told you what will happen if not ...'

I swallowed, remembering the half-truth I'd told earlier. At least I'd thought to say that the hiding place for the guns got changed on a regular basis.

'So Djounsou wants me as his secret weapon?' I said.

Carson nodded. 'It's funny, really, seeing as Geri went to such lengths to keep your existence a secret. That's why all the charges against me were dropped, you know. Because so much of the evidence would have had to come from you and the others and Geri didn't want you exposed.'

'Can I see them – the others?'

'The girls, yes. Nico's locked away somewhere else but, yes, the girls ... come with me.'

Carson took me round the corner to some sort of communications room, full of desks and monitors. An armed guard stood in the doorway. Two more were inside the room.

'As you can see,' Carson said, 'there are cameras everywhere, the highest security ... and armed guards at all the exits.'

I peered more closely into the room. A row of black-and-white monitors showed silent CCTV from about ten different places. Several screens showed empty corridors and unused rooms. I could see Nico, bound and gagged, in one room and the girls in another. The three of them were standing in a huddle, like they were chatting in low voices. From this distance none of them looked beaten up or obviously injured.

'That's enough,' Carson ordered.

He took me along the corridor to the room at the end, unlocked it and shoved me inside. The girls were there, still huddled together, like they had been when I'd seen them on the monitor. Now I was seeing them in the flesh, it was obvious Ketty and Luz had both been crying.

Before either of the others could move, Ketty raced towards me and flung herself into my arms.

'Oh, Ed, you're okay!'

I hugged her back, hard. Over her shoulder I could see Dylan, standing with her arms folded. Luz leaned against the wall, watching me, then slid down so she was sitting, huddled against the concrete, her thin arms wrapped round her knees. I wanted to go to her, but I also wanted to be hugging Ketty.

To be honest, in spite of everything that had happened to us, I have to admit it felt good to have two girls caring about me.

Ketty stepped away from me. 'What did they make you do?' she said.

I told them about having to mind-read Tsonga and what Carson had said about me being handed over to General Djounsou.

'He said there were plans for Nico, too. He's locked up in one of the other cells. Have you seen him?'

'Not since we got off that freakin' boat,' Dylan said.

172

Ketty's golden-brown eyes widened with concern. 'Haven't you tried to communicate with him, Ed?' she said.

I shook my head, suddenly feeling guilty.

'By the way,' Dylan said, 'there's a camera above the door.'

'I know,' I said. 'There's one in my room too, but I've seen the monitors. They can't hear us.'

'Good, because we've already been talking about how we can get out of here,' Dylan said. 'And I've got an idea.'

'Yeah, but we need a proper plan, Dylan.' Ketty glanced at me, her eyebrows raised.

'It *is* a proper plan, Ketty,' Dylan snarled. 'It's a *good* plan. And it's all we've got, unless you've come up with something based on your latest vision.' She paused, opening her eyes wide in pretend shock. 'Oh, no. Wait. I forgot. You haven't *had* a freakin' vision.'

'Your ability isn't any more helpful than mine,' Ketty snapped. 'And your plan is rubbish.'

Despite the fact that they were both talking quietly, Luz covered her ears.

'Shut up, both of you,' I said.

Ketty and Dylan stopped glaring at each other and turned to face me. Ketty looked a little shamefaced, Dylan just raised her eyebrows.

'*What* did you say?' she said.

'Having a go at each other won't help anything,' I said. 'Plus, it's upsetting Luz.' I pointed to where Luz sat, head bowed, ears still covered, in the corner of the room.

Dylan's green eyes narrowed. 'Well, Ed, I'm very sorry

about that but, gee, I guess I'm just a little bit stressed by everything. Apart from the fact that we're freakin' prisoners here, they keep taking blood from me and I *hate* needles.'

'Be quiet and look at me,' I said. It suddenly occurred to me that just because the security monitors didn't pick up sound, didn't mean the room wasn't bugged, and I needed a chance to tell all the girls about my contact with Amy – and how Geri would surely be on her way to rescue us soon – without taking any risks that Carson's men might be listening in.

Dylan hesitated a second, then raised her eyes. *Whoosh.*

The inside of Dylan's mind felt like a taut muscle, stretched to snapping point. Residual anger and resentment seemed to overlay all her thoughts and feelings and yet I sensed a huge vulnerability underneath.

Listen, Ed, she thought-spoke in her imperious way. *We need to jump the next guard who appears. Make a run for it while the door's unlocked. If we get out, we can bring back help for Nico.*

Wait . . .

No, listen. Dylan's thought-speech was insistent. *When the guard comes back, you hold him with your mind-reading while we tie him up. We've linked our bras together to make a sort of rope. It's not great, but we can fasten his hands to the door handle. It'll give us a few minutes and—*

That's insane. A million images of bras and guards and beds filled my head. I blushed, hoping Dylan wasn't able to see any of them. *It's far too risky. I've seen the CCTV monitors in this place – there's millions of them and the guards have guns.*

We have to do something.

I already am, I said, eagerly. *I've managed to contact my sister, Amy, by remote telepathy. She's going to tell Geri what's happening. I'm contacting her again in a few hours. She should have found Geri by then.*

I could feel Dylan's mood shift as I spoke, hope surging up through the cynicism, then fading as she checked herself.

I didn't think you could do mind-reading remotely? she thought-spoke. *I mean, Ketty said what you did on the boat, but you couldn't do that before, could you?*

No, but I can do it now. Just be patient. And don't think about us trying to escape on our own. It'd be suicide.

I broke the connection, then thought-spoke the same information to Ketty.

As I was finishing up, Dylan hissed in my ear. 'Stop, Carson's coming.'

I broke off immediately, just as the footsteps stopped and the door opened. I glanced over my shoulder. Carson was standing in the doorway. 'I need you to come with me, now, kiddo,' he said.

Damn. I hadn't had a chance to speak to Luz. I turned towards her. Ketty grabbed my arm.

'Try the remote thing with Nico,' she whispered. 'Find out where he is ... if he's okay ...'

Nodding, I hurried over to where Luz was still sitting.

She jumped up and put her arms round me. She was trembling.

'I scared, Eds,' she whispered in my ear.

My stomach cartwheeled. 'It'll be okay,' I whispered back. 'You'll be all right, I promise.'

'*Come on*, Ed,' Carson ordered from the door. 'General Djounsou wants to meet you. And he's not a man to be kept waiting.'

19: THE GENERAL

The room Djounsou was in was heavily guarded and in another part of the complex. Carson had led me through a bewildering maze of corridors to get there. I'd kept my eyes open for Nico, but saw no sign of him.

Carson spoke as we walked, giving me instructions on how to behave.

'Djounsou took over the country through a military coup several months ago, but he's not secure in his position and he sees enemies all around him. Don't try to get too close to him – his guards won't like it.' He stopped outside a hefty fire door. 'This is it – as far as I go. Djounsou doesn't want to see me again – you're on your own, kiddo.'

He pushed the door open. Heart pounding, I walked through. I was in some kind of waiting room, with another door opposite. Two soldiers stood on either side of it – big men with big guns. As soon as they saw me, one of them turned and rapped on the door. A woman opened it. She was young and black and traditionally dressed in a yellow and black swathe of material. She glanced at me, then beckoned me through.

The next room was another waiting room, but much more luxuriously furnished with plush red velvet chairs arranged around an ornate stone fireplace. The woman indicated I should sit in one of the chairs. As I did, she vanished through another door.

I sat for a few seconds, intimidated by the unexpected formality of the room. A gold clock stood on the mantelpiece opposite me. Its loud tick seemed to underline the tension in the atmosphere. And then the woman reappeared, flanked by two more guards. Both had rifles slung over their backs and handguns in their holsters. They stood back, to allow a third man to walk between them. He was shorter, older and fatter than them both – in a plain khaki uniform, with medals pinned to his chest. Despite his slightly stooped posture and the way his stomach swelled over his belt, I had no doubt this was Djounsou. His presence filled the room.

'Ed?' His smile showed a row of startlingly white teeth. 'I am General Djounsou.'

I stood up. Both guards immediately stepped forward, guns raised. I sat back down.

'Is okay,' Djounsou barked. 'I will sit too.'

He positioned himself in the armchair opposite me. His bulky frame seemed too big for the chair, his arms lying like logs along the slender velvet armrests.

'I have seen your powers of ... telepathy,' he went on. His voice was deep and accented and as formal as the room we were sitting in. 'What you do is impressive. I would like a demonstration for myself ... *on* myself.'

'You?' I said, my voice quaking. 'You want me to read *your* mind?'

'Exactly.' Djounsou chuckled. 'Show me, but please get no ideas about abusing this privilege. My guards like to shoot.' His laugh deepened. The woman, who was leaning on the back of his chair, laughed too. I got the impression that Djounsou had made this particular joke many times before.

I swallowed. There wasn't much choice. I lifted my eyes. I held Djounsou in my gaze for a few seconds, taking in the hardness of his bloodshot brown eyes, then dived in.

A clinical, ruthless mind lay in front of me. Guarded, but then I would have expected that. Like anyone who knew what I could do, Djounsou was trying hard to keep certain information away from me. It would have been easy for me to get him to reveal it, but I didn't probe. Instead I watched the thoughts that danced across the surface of his mind. These were mostly fairly superficial ... lust for some young girl in his secretarial staff ... the goat stew he'd had for lunch that kept repeating on him ... how he hated the thin walls of the compound that carried noise and disturbed him whenever he wanted to sit quietly.

What do you want me to do now? I thought-spoke, feeling awkward.

Djounsou's mind rushed with the excitement of realising what I was doing.

So this is how ... You are speaking without sound. Most impressive. Tell me what you see.

179

I hesitated, not sure how to respond. No one had ever asked me to describe their mind before. Obviously, I kept these thoughts hidden from the general.

Er ... it's ... you have a strong mind ... very powerful, I thought-spoke, hoping to flatter him, then added – in case he wanted more detail – *and, er ... you're annoyed because the thin walls of the compound make it noisy ...*

Yes, yes. Djounsou seemed delighted. *The walls are indeed most hollow and flimsy. Can you see any of my other thoughts?*

He meant the ones he was attempting to hide. I hesitated, wondering how far to probe. A week or so ago we'd been after a criminal back in England called Damian Foster. When I'd tried to push into his thoughts and feelings, Foster had been able to use my ability to hook into him telepathically to hold me, trapped, in his own mind. After mind-reading Foster I'd been sick, partly through the effort it had taken to break away from him, but mostly from the fear of having him control me like that.

It hadn't happened before or since, but the experience had left me wary.

I pushed a little way into Djounsou's thoughts. He definitely didn't possess the sinewy mental strength that I'd felt in Foster. I mean, I sensed Djounsou was clearly hugely arrogant but he also seemed straightforward, unused to any need for manipulation or mental flexibility. In fact, he gave every impression of a man used to getting his way through brute force – or the threat of it.

This was not an entirely comforting observation.

If you give me permission to read your thoughts, I would be happy to do so, I thought-spoke cautiously.

Go ahead. I could sense the tension ... the anticipation, in Djounsou's mind.

I took a deep breath and plunged in.

Pushing hard into someone's thoughts is a bit like being in the middle of the sea and watching all the waves around you, then picking on a single wave and catching it like a surfer does, riding it into the shore.

Just like real waves, every thought is a different shape and size and duration – and yet, there's something that connects them all, just like all waves are fundamentally curves of moving water.

I rode a thought very close to the surface of Djounsou's mind. His curiosity about my ability ... his hope that it would help him. I pushed through, into the next thought. Images of power and violence mingled with a terrible fear – almost a paranoia – about various enemies. I got a snatch of memory about a man Djounsou had killed, a knife slitting across his throat. Horrified, I tore away from that to another memory – Djounsou driving through villages, gun strapped to his back, at the head of a convoy of army vehicles. He stood proud in his open-top jeep, his hand raised to acknowledge the rows of people cheering his arrival. Then Djounsou in the centre of a group of soldiers, entertaining everyone with beer and jokes.

I sensed Djounsou caught up in his own curiosity about what I was able to see, but at the same time appalled at how much insight I was getting. He was going to tell me to stop any second.

I plunged into a new wave of thought. *Yes.* Here was his plan for using me to interrogate his enemies, built on his fear of the rebellion led by Tsonga.

With a jolt I realised how absolutely Djounsou was determined to quash that rebellion, whatever it took.

What are you planning to do with Tsonga and the people hiding weapons in Mahore? I thought-spoke the question, knowing that, in trying to deny me the answer, Djounsou would inadvertently reveal it.

No. Stop this. Stop. Make an example of the rebels. This is too far, I order you to stop. Round them up and kill them.

I broke the connection and shrank back, horrified. So Tsonga *was* going to die. Which meant his little daughter, Victoria, was going to die too.

Djounsou, freed from my mental grip, roared with fury. He leaped to his feet and pointed at the closest guard. 'Gun,' he ordered.

The guard thrust the handgun from his holster into Djounsou's hand, then stepped smartly back.

Djounsou grabbed it and thrust it against my throat.

I froze, all my attention now on the cold metal pressing against my neck.

'I told you to stop.' Djounsou cocked the gun. 'Now you will pay.'

20: THE KILLING

'Don't, please,' I stammered.

Djounsou pressed the gun harder against my throat. 'Give me one good reason why I should not pull this trigger. *No one* can be seen to disobey me. *No one.*'

Fear shot through me like fire, consuming me.

'No one saw,' I said desperately. 'And I can help you find out stuff ... er, information about your enemies. Remember, like you said?'

Djounsou hesitated. The press of the gun lightened against my neck.

'What I did with you – reading your thoughts – was a fraction of what I could do with one of the rebels fighting against you,' I went on. 'Think how powerful that would make you.'

Djounsou was right up in my face. His eyes opened so wide you could see the whites all round the iris. I hated myself for offering to do his dirty work like this, but what other option did I have? I comforted myself with the thought that once I'd made contact with Amy again, Geri would surely race to rescue us – and Djounsou could be stopped.

'You're a great man,' I said, quietly. 'Keeping me around can only make you greater.'

Djounsou's face softened. He chuckled. 'This is true.' To my intense relief, he withdrew his gun and held it out to one of the guards. As he did so, the rest of the room came back into my awareness – the guards and the woman in her yellow and black traditional dress, all watching us intently ... the fireplace ... the ornate ticking clock on the mantelpiece.

'This is your one and only chance,' Djounsou went on. 'Betray me again and there will not be a second.'

Djounsou stood up and beckoned for one of the guards to take me away. Without speaking he turned his back and vanished through the door he'd used earlier, the other guard and the woman trailing in his wake.

I was taken back to my corridor and locked inside my cell, feeling shaken but relieved. I sat on the bed for a second, letting what had just happened sink in. I had no idea what time it was, though the sky outside my window was still dark.

I lay down. As soon as it was dawn I would try contacting my sister again, see if she'd managed to get hold of Geri.

In the meantime, where was Nico? I felt a stab of guilt – he'd been kept away from the rest of us for hours now. Plus, I'd promised Ketty I'd attempt to reach him. I closed my eyes and focused, trying to relax into what I was doing.

184

I felt myself flickering in and out of his mind, but only for a few seconds. Then ... *whoosh* ... I was there, inside Nico's head, feeling the stress and anxiety of his current state of mind.

Nico? I'd forgotten how surprisingly intense his mind felt. More brooding and troubled than you'd expect from the way he showed off most of the time.

Ed? Nico's thought-speech sounded entirely astonished. *What ... how ...?*

I smiled to myself at his confusion. *Remote telepathy. I've been working on it for a while. Ketty helped. Where are you? Are you okay?*

I'm fine. Is Ketty with you?

I could hear the concern in his voice ... and the slightest edge of jealousy.

No, but I've seen her – and Dylan and Luz. We're all good.

Thanks. Say, Ed, what you're doing is amazing.

I bit my lip. That was so like Nico. He'd give you a million reasons to get annoyed with him, then be nice, just when you least expected it.

Who else have you contacted like this?

Just you and Ketty. And my sister, Amy.

You have to try contacting Geri.

Yes, I know. I'm on it. Er, Nico, I saw you on one of the monitors here, but where are you?

In a cell. Underground, I think ... there's no natural light ... no furniture – they only come in to give me food and empty the piss bucket.

Nice.

Yeah, it's the frigging Ritz. At least the bucket's something to practise telekinesis with. I can control it now so I can tip it as far as it'll go without anything spilling. Even with a blindfold on.

I wasn't sure if he was joking or not, but before I had time to respond, Nico's thought-speech softened.

Is Ketty really okay?

She's fine. I hesitated. *She's worried about you, though.*

Right.

Nico was trying to make his thoughts sound gruff and dismissive, but I could sense his genuine longing for her. I didn't want Nico to get any hint that I was aware of that, so I quickly explained exactly how I'd contacted my sister and how I was expecting to be able to communicate with Geri within the next few hours.

That's brilliant. I could feel Nico's mood lift as he listened to me.

We thought-spoke a little more, then I ended the connection.

I must have fallen asleep, because the next thing I remember was the sound of the door being unlocked. I sat bolt upright as one of the guards came in with Luz.

The guard pushed her inside, then shut and locked the door again. I blinked stupidly at her, still half-asleep, and she smiled – a sad, beautiful smile that made my stomach flip over. I hesitated for a second, then walked over to where she stood at the door, my heart beating fast. I was pretty sure there was a blind spot there that the security cameras couldn't see.

We stood in the doorway, facing each other.

'Man say is okay me see you,' she said softly.

I stared at her.

She smiled again. 'Do speaking in my head, Eds.'

My heart was thumping so loudly in the silent room I thought she must be able to hear. I met her eyes. *Whoosh.*

I did remote telepathy with Nico, I thought-spoke in a gabble, trying not to give away just how transfixed I was by her presence. *He's okay, and in an hour or so I'm going to try and contact the woman who took us to the camp and tell her what's going on. Then she'll rescue all of us.*

Que? No entiendo.

She didn't understand. I searched my scrambled brain for the Spanish I needed. *Er . . . salvamento pronto. Rescue, soon.*

Luz's mind flooded with relief and admiration. *You are good peoples, Eds, I believe you help.* She held back for a second, as if the next thought she wanted to consciously express was something significant. And then she thought-spoke it: *I likes you, Eds. Mucho.*

I could feel myself blushing. Was she coming on to me?

For a second I imagined what Nico would say if he were here: 'Of course she's frigging coming on to you, man. How big a hint are you looking for?'

I broke the connection and took her hand, then was gripped with doubt. Suppose I'd misread that? Suppose Luz had just

187

meant she wanted to be friends? I stared at the floor, as Luz moved a fraction closer to me.

'Eds?' she said, very softly. 'Ven aqui.' *Come here.*

Okay. I tried to speak, but my throat was too dry. Instead I did as she asked and shuffled closer. She tilted her head up to me and I bent my head down to hers and then I knew it was going to happen and I closed my eyes and we kissed.

It was amazing.

I'd kissed girls before, of course ... well, one or two ... but never anyone that looked quite like Luz. I suddenly realised what people mean when they say something good is 'blinding' because that's what that kiss was – like it took everything else in the world away.

It went on for ages, too. In the end, Luz pulled away.

'Talk me, Eds.'

With a glance at the camera, I grabbed my blanket off the bed and brought it over to the door. We sat against the wall, wrapped up together, chatting as the sky lightened into pearl-grey swirls.

I asked Luz why she'd been brought to see me. She said she'd asked if she could and the guard had said yes. I didn't understand why, but I wasn't complaining.

Luz asked me about 'the other boy' and his ability to move objects with his mind. I explained Nico had been born with a Gift, like me, then braced myself for the inevitable comments that most girls make about how gorgeous Nico looks. But Luz just smiled and changed the subject to why Carson had brought us here.

'He wants to sell our abilities to men like Djounsou, who

can use me to find out information from people.' I paused, wanting to reassure her. 'At least it's just about the money. Carson isn't interested in killing people – certainly not in hurting kids.'

Luz stared at me. 'Eds, this is no true,' she said earnestly. 'Carson helps Djounsou make war, no?'

I nodded. 'Yes, he does, but ...'

'And war causes children no parents ... orphans ... and refug ... refug ...'

'Refugees,' I finished for her.

'Yes, so Carson makes children very poor and very sad and very without homes. Just like me.'

I sat back, thinking it through. It was true, though I'd never thought about it before. The war that Djounsou was waging and Carson was supporting *was* creating child victims – vulnerable enough to end up being trafficked in just the same way that Luz and the other street kids had been in Spain.

'You're right,' I whispered. 'But don't be scared. I'll make sure you're safe, I promise.'

Luz smiled and, soon after that, we stopped talking altogether.

It was bliss. Eventually I felt Luz's head grow heavy on my chest and her breathing even out. I closed my eyes as she slept. Maybe I should get a little sleep too. Then, in the morning, it would be time to try and contact Amy again – and Geri.

Wham! The door slammed open with a huge bang. It hit the wall right next to where we were huddled. I jerked awake, out of a deep sleep, just in time to see Luz being hauled up by her hair and pulled away from me.

'Stand up, you little bastard!' Carson towered over me.

I struggled to my feet as he grabbed my arm.

'What?'

'Silence!' Carson barked.

I looked over his shoulder at the guard holding Luz. He had a gun pointing into her side.

'This way.' Carson dragged me down the corridor. He unlocked the girls' room, then threw me inside. Luz was hurled in after me.

A fist thumped against the switch and the naked overhead light glared on.Across the room, both Ketty and Dylan reared up out of their blankets.

I blinked in the sudden brightness, completely disorientated. What was going on?

Carson stomped over and grabbed my arm again, so tight it hurt. He was wearing sunglasses.

'Hey!' Ketty yelled.

'Let go of him,' Dylan added.

'Shut up.' Carson shook my arm, then prodded me in the chest.

'You lied to me about what you saw in Tsonga's mind.'

I shook my head. *Oh no, oh no, oh no.*

Across the room, Luz backed away towards her own mattress, in the far corner. She looked petrified.

'Speak!' Carson ordered.

'I am. I . . . I told you the truth.'

Over Carson's shoulder I could see Djounsou, flanked by two guards, come into the room. Like Carson, all three were in sunglasses. On the other side of the doorway stood Tsonga, his hands tied behind his back. A fresh bruise made a dark red mark across his cheek. He looked exhausted.

'No, Ed, you lied,' Carson spat. 'You told us that the weapons in Mahore were last seen in a hut with a blue wall and a red flag on the road west out of town.'

'They move the weapons all the time,' I said, desperately. 'I said that too.'

'Yes.' Carson was breathing heavily, his face contorted with rage. 'But the thing is, Ed, we know you made up the hut.'

'What ... how?'

'There *is* no hut with a blue wall and a red flag on the road west out of town.'

A tense silence spread across the room. I glanced at Tsonga. Hadn't he specifically told me to pretend that's where the weapons were? His expression was a mix of defiance and guilt. And then he met my eyes and I dived into his mind.

Why did you tell me to say the weapons were in a hut that doesn't exist? I thought-spoke.

I was trying to protect my family – my village. I could not say the guns were in any place. Anyone found in whatever building I said would be killed. Ed, please, you must help my daughter. She is everything I have ... my life.

I broke the connection, furious. I'd tried to give Tsonga

191

a chance and he'd just made things worse for both of us. I glanced at the general. He was watching me, his expression behind his sunglasses impassive.

'I warned you, Ed.' Djounsou shook his head. 'You already had your one and only chance.'

Carson raised his gun and held it against my head. 'Tell us where the weapons are *really* being hidden.'

My stomach tightened into a tense knot. What should I do? Admit I knew all along that the weapons were in the church in Mahore – which was an admission of the guilt I'd just denied and likely to get me shot? Or carry on claiming I had no idea – and probably get shot anyway?

I forced myself to speak. 'I'm sorry,' I said, my voice barely more than a squeak, 'I must have made a mistake. Let me mind-read Tsonga again and try to find out where they are.'

I knew I was taking a calculated risk in not coming clean, but it seemed the best option. At least this way I could pretend to see the information for the first time.

Unfortunately, my gamble didn't pay off. Carson pushed the gun against my temple and roared. 'There was no bloody mistake! You lied to us and now you're lying about lying.'

I glanced round the room. Ketty and Dylan were huddled together on the floor, watching what was going on with wide, scared eyes. Luz was still sitting on her mattress, her body trembling. I reached out my hand instinctively towards her, trying to reassure her.

Big mistake.

192

Carson had followed my movement.

'Yes,' he said, slowly. 'An excellent choice, kiddo. No one will care about *her*. Except you.' He walked over and trained his gun on Luz.

Luz gasped and shrank away, pressing herself against the wall.

'Stop!' I rushed up to them, my heart like thunder in my ears. He couldn't hurt her. He *couldn't*. Luz had done nothing wrong.

The confession spewed out of me like vomit. 'Don't take it out on her. You're right, I did see where the weapons are in Mahore. Tsonga's brother is hiding them in the church basement – St Luke's Church.'

Carson lowered his gun. Across the room Tsonga's face contorted with grief.

'My little Victoria,' he wailed.

Suddenly I saw what an impossible position he was in. I met his eyes, consumed with guilt. If Tsonga and his brother were killed, then Victoria would become an orphan – perhaps even a refugee – without a home or anyone to protect her.

Just like Luz.

I'm so sorry, I thought-spoke. *Please understand I had to tell them. He was going to kill my friend.*

Please help Victoria. Tsonga's plea pierced through me. *Please save Victoria. She is just a child.*

I will. I promise. I broke the connection again and looked round the room.

Djounsou was in the doorway barking orders at his private soldiers, telling them to contact their comrades in Mahore.

193

'They must find the weapons in the church, round up Tsonga's brother and the rest of his family, then wait.' Djounsou checked his watch. 'I will be there in two hours.'

I gazed round. Ketty and Dylan were watching us, still huddled together across the room. Luz was shaking, pressed up against the wall. I knelt down and put my hand on her arm.

'Do you still want this one?' Carson said, indicating me.

Djounsou slowly nodded. 'Yes. I do not think he is lying now. It seems as if he has *almost* learned his lesson.'

I held my breath. What did that mean?

'You're right.' Carson said. 'About both things. He is telling the truth now, but he still needs to be punished for lying to us before.'

He raised the gun and pointed it at Luz's head again.

She shrank further away. My hand fell from her arm.

'No!' I said. 'I told you what you wanted to know.'

'But not in time,' Carson said, not taking his eyes off Luz. 'Remember, Ed. This is *your* punishment. *You* did this.'

I froze. This couldn't be happening.

'No,' Luz sobbed, 'no, por favor!' She spun wildly to face me. 'Eds, help—'

The gun exploded as I reached for her. Luz jerked back against the wall, then slumped to the mattress. Across the room, Ketty screamed.

I stared at Luz's body. It was bent at an impossible angle, her hair fanned out over the mattress, her arm trailing onto the floor.

I couldn't take it in.

And then the world came back into focus. And I knew that nothing in my life would ever be the same, because the girl I had kissed, and promised to help, with the silky hair and the beautiful sea-green eyes, was lying on the floor beside me, dead.

21: DECISION

Ketty's scream died away and a terrible silence filled the room.

Carson stood, panting, staring down at Luz's body. Everyone else was frozen in the moment, which seemed to stretch inside my head, as if I'd been sitting, gazing at Luz's lifeless body for days rather than seconds. Blood was seeping out from the back of her head. I watched it, mesmerised, unable to take in what I was seeing. A strand of hair had fallen across her face. I knelt to brush it away, then glanced up.

Ketty and Dylan were staring at me, their faces stricken. Across the room, Djounsou stood, apparently unmoved, but Tsonga was weeping, his body heaving in great sobs as he stared at Luz.

She's dead. The words went through my head, but didn't seem to connect with the reality of what lay in front of me.

'Stupid girl, getting in the way.' Carson curled his lip in disgust.

'NO!' The yell tore out of me like a bullet. And somehow I was on my feet, hurling myself at him. Anger like I'd never known before – a red haze all around me – swallowed me up. I punched and shouted – totally off my head. The two guards started threatening and tugging at me, but I didn't stop. Couldn't.

Carson punched me in the gut. I doubled over, then lunged back at him.

In the background I was dimly aware of Ketty's screams and Dylan's yells and, above them both, Djounsou's thunderous command: 'Do not hurt him.'

I have no idea how long the struggle lasted. In the end, I felt someone grip my arm above the elbow, then the familiar ratchety noise of the stun gun. A searing pain in my shoulder and the world went black.

When I woke it was almost daylight – the dawn sky was a soft grey-blue and the dark pearly swirls from earlier had faded to pale pink. I was back in my cell, lying on the narrow camp bed. My head throbbed and my wrists and ankles felt sore. For a second I lay there, completely disoriented. I moved a little – but my hands and feet were tied up. Why?

And then I remembered. I struggled to sit up, my head filled with the image of Luz's dead body. For a moment I thought I was going to be sick.

I sat on the edge of the bed, feet firmly planted on the floor, and took a few deep breaths. I couldn't have been out for that long. From the look of the sky outside, no more than half an hour had passed since I went into the girls' room.

Again, an image of Luz's slumped body flashed into my head. I saw her face, turning to me, her mouth opening to speak. *Ed, help me ...*

I closed my eyes, unable to bear it.

She had died asking for my help, just as she had lived believing I would help her.

What had Carson said to me? *You did this.*

It was true. I felt sick. I'd promised to help Luz and, instead, I had led her into terrible danger. I had insisted Carson brought her with us and now ...

The door opened. I caught a flash of a guard's uniform, then Nico – blindfolded and bound by metal chains at the wrists and ankles – was pushed into the room.

The door shut. Nico stumbled forwards. 'Hello?' His voice sounded weaker and more scared than I'd ever heard it. 'Is anyone there?'

'Just me, Ed,' I said.

'Phew.' Nico relaxed a little. 'They've moved me. Need my room for something – it sounded like they were leaving a body down there, but I couldn't be sure.'

He didn't know.

'Right.' The word came out like I was being strangled.

'You don't sound very pleased to see me,' Nico said, with a terse grin. 'God, these frigging chains they've put on me. I have no idea how to undo them – it feels like they're frigging welded together.'

198

I said nothing.

'Ed, has something happened? The girls are all right, aren't they?'

I bit my lip and stared at the ground.

Nico sat down in the middle of the room. 'Ed?' His voice was suddenly tense. 'What's going on?'

I told him about Luz, keeping my eyes on the dirty concrete floor at my feet and my explanation as brief and factual as possible. 'So afterwards,' I said, flatly, 'I went mad and attacked Carson and the guards knocked me out. I just this minute woke up.'

Silence. I looked up. Nico's face behind the blindfold was pale.

'Oh, God,' he whispered. 'He actually *killed* her?'

I swallowed, the image of Luz's lifeless body forcing itself into my mind again.

'Yes,' I said. 'I'm guessing it's her body they've put in your room.'

Silence again. 'What about Geri?' Nico said. 'Have you made contact with her?'

'Not yet,' I said. Everything that had happened earlier had knocked my plan to make contact with Amy – and therefore Geri Paterson – out of my head.

'It's even more important now, Ed,' Nico insisted. 'Now we know how far Carson's prepared to go.'

I suddenly remembered Tsonga – and Djounsou's mission to punish the rebels in Mahore. He'd told his soldiers he'd be there in two hours, less than thirty minutes ago.

Here was my chance to keep my promise to help Tsonga's daughter. If I could just contact Geri she would be able to rescue us *and* stop Djounsou murdering Tsonga's family and the other rebels. I'd failed to save Luz. I *had* to help Tsonga.

I took a deep breath. 'Okay,' I said.

Nico lay back on the floor. I tried to focus on my sister, Amy. Would I be able to connect with her a second time? After all, the remote mind-reading hadn't worked with anyone else apart from Nico and Ketty.

I slowed my breathing and pictured Amy's pale face and blue eyes.

With a whoosh, I was there. I recognised Amy's mind straight away – the same high-pitched level of hysteria as before.

Hi, Amy.

Ed? The whirlwind of emotion that was Amy's mind spun faster. *Ohmigod, ohmigod, it's you, it's really you.*

Yes, did you tell Mum and Dad? Did they get Geri?

Yes. They're all here. Geri's been here all night, waiting.

I sighed with relief. *Okay, Amy, I need you to tell her exactly what I tell you. All right?*

I don't like her, Ed. She looks at me like I'm some stupid little kid. And she's been really rude to Mum and Dad too.

I know, but, Amy, this is important. Blake Carson has captured us. We're okay but being held prisoner in a compound, somewhere in North Africa, near a place called Mahore. Tell her now, then tell me you're done.

Ohmigod, ohmigod. Okay.

I waited while Amy spoke out loud to Geri. I could hear the echo of her voice as it sounded in her head, but not anything going on in the wider world, which meant I couldn't hear Geri's reply. After what felt like a long time, Amy was back.

Ed?

What did she say?

She said I had to tell you that the four of you should attempt to get yourselves out of the compound and—

What? I couldn't believe what I was hearing. *Isn't she coming to rescue us?*

She says she has no idea where you are – that her contacts at Interpol don't know where Carson's compound is. That the satellite pictures over the area aren't giving any useful clues. She wants you to get to safety, then contact her – to say where the compound is. She'll send people to pick you up – and to deal with Carson.

But . . . I could barely formulate my thoughts into anything coherent enough to communicate. *Getting out of here without help is impossible. Tell her we can't do it.* I explained how Carson had killed Luz and about Djounsou and what he'd made me find out from Tsonga and how Tsonga's family and village were now in terrible danger.

It took a while. Amy kept stopping me, uncertain of the names, then telling Geri small bits of information at a time. Geri's reply was much more succinct. Through Amy, she told me:

I'm sorry about the girl, but that just shows you what Carson is capable of. As for Djounsou, he's small fry in global terms and I don't want you sidetracked. I will report what you've said to the Foreign Office, but they're already well aware of his activities in the region.

Then why aren't they doing anything about it?

It's not our problem, Geri's response came back. *I'm sorry you're caught up in this, Ed, but you need to stay focused on getting to safety as fast as possible . . .*

So that's what it came down to – Geri didn't care about Tsonga and his family and she certainly didn't care about Luz. She didn't even really care about me and Nico, Dylan and Ketty. We were all just pawns in her game.

Well, Tsonga had asked for my help to save his daughter and I had promised to give it. I was never going to make that promise again – to anyone – and fail.

I ended the connection and told Nico – using remote telepathy, in case Carson had bugged the room – what Geri had said. He was as shocked as I was.

So we have to get out of here alone and find a safe place to contact Geri.

Yes, but we're not doing that.

What? Nico thought-spoke. *What are we going to do, then, Ed?*

I gritted my teeth, Luz's lifeless body filling my mind again. *We can't just desert Tsonga and the people in Mahore. Djounsou's going to kill Tsonga's daughter. We have to at least try to stop him.*

Ed, have you gone mad? How the hell are we going to do that? Djounsou's got a frigging army!

We go to Mahore. Prevent the killings.

What? How are we going to get there? And even if we do, it's a suicide mission.

We've got powers. You were all keen about being part of The Medusa Project. Well, this is what we do. We fight crime. We stop bad people like Carson and Djounsou from starting wars and creating innocent victims – like Tsonga's daughter – because ordinary people can't *do it themselves. But we can ... between us we've got amazing skills.*

Okay. Listen, Ed ... Even if we can *get ourselves to Mahore, how are we going to stop Djounsou's army from killing the rebels?*

I don't know yet, but we will. Somehow. I took a deep breath. *There's something else. If we manage to get out and tell Geri where Carson's compound is, there's a big chance that he won't be here when she arrives. We have to make sure he follows us to Mahore. Then we can be certain she'll have a chance of finding him – and dealing with him.*

Nico's thoughts and feelings swirled up in his head – a mix of intense emotions. He thought I was mad. He thought I was brave. He was astonished I was capable of coming up with – let alone acting on – such a plan.

Never mind all that, I cut across his thoughts. *Djounsou's men are probably already on their way to Mahore. They'll have had almost an hour's start on us. Which means our first priority is to escape from this room.*

Escape? Nico's thought-speech now sounded completely bewildered. *But I'm chained and blindfolded and you must be tied up too.*

I know. I paused for a second. *Here's what I think we should do.*

22: CORNERED

We were ready when the guard arrived with our food. As he pushed the door open, I held my breath. What we were going to do would require split-second timing.

As I'd feared, the guard was wearing sunglasses, like Carson and Djounsou had been earlier. That would make what we were planning even trickier. He put the tray, containing two bowls, cups and spoons, on the floor in front of Nico, then stood back.

Nico groped for the food. He found one of the bowls and fell on it, grabbing a spoon and shovelling in the contents – some sort of watery stew. It was clearly hard for him to coordinate the movement with his hands tied, but the guard didn't seem to have any intention of helping by untying him.

He was a stocky guy – one of the unsmiling men I'd glimpsed through the doorway of the communications room round the corner. I cleared my throat.

'What about me?' I said.

The guard's bunch of keys slapped against his side as he

turned to me, then picked up the second bowl and shoved it into my hands. Nico was still scooping up stew like he hadn't eaten for a week.

'Eat,' the guard ordered.

I nodded, then raised my arms. 'I can't eat with chains on.'

'Tough.'

I swallowed. 'Maybe if you took off your sunglasses you'd be able to see to undo me.'

'Keep quiet.'

This was Nico's cue. He held his bound hands outstretched towards the man, clearly working out where he was from his voice. Then he telekinetically whipped the sunglasses from the man's face. Before the man had time to react, I jumped up, right into his face, forcing him to meet my eyes.

Whoosh. The man's mind filled with shock and fear.

What . . . what's happening . . . how . . .

I sensed the man's personality – dull and plodding with a cruel streak. I let him expend his energy in confused raging, while focusing all mine on holding his mind in place.

'Over here, Nico, the key's on his belt.'

Nico shuffled towards us, feeling his way with his hands. As he got closer I reached out and yanked off his blindfold, still keeping my gaze on the guard. Able to see at last, Nico chucked my blanket over the camera, then unhooked the key from the guard's belt and undid first his own hands and feet, then mine.

'So that's how they work,' he muttered. 'That's a really clever design.'

'Come on,' I said. My heart was beating fast. Once the guys in the communications room noticed the monitor showing us was covered, they'd be here in seconds.

As Nico fastened the chains round the guard's hands and feet, I felt the man's resistance to my mind control increase.

It's not a part of my ability that I like, being able to control people's actions. It works in kind of a weird way. Obviously I can't stop people from thinking and feeling whatever they're going to feel, but I can prevent thoughts which are basically instructions to the body from getting through.

'Done,' Nico said, fastening his blindfold around the guard's mouth.

I broke the connection with the guard at last, pushing him down onto the bed.

We raced to the door, ducking under the blanket that was still covering the camera lens. How much time did we have before more guards arrived from the communications room to see what had happened?

We ran out into the corridor.

'Where are the girls?' Nico asked.

'Down here.' I pointed to the room where, such a short time ago, Luz had been killed. I shivered.

We ran down the corridor. Shouts were already echoing towards us from the communications room round the corner – presumably the security guards had just seen that the camera in our cell had gone dark. *God*, were we going to have enough time to reach the girls?

Nico skidded to a halt at their door. With a single twist of his hand, it flew open. Dylan and Ketty jumped up from where they were sitting on the far side of the room. I didn't want to look at the place where Luz had died, but my eyes took me there anyway. The mattress was gone – as indeed was all the furniture in the room – only a bloodstain on the wall was left.

My heart thumped a furious beat against my ribs, as Ketty ran across the room and flung herself into Nico's arms. Sobbing, she reached out for my hand.

'Oh, Ed,' she whispered, 'you're safe … you're both safe …'

At that moment the screech of a high-pitched alarm started. Footsteps sounded in the distance.

Dylan's eyes were wide. 'What—?'

'Nico!' I shouted. 'The lock.'

Nico spun round and locked us in the room. 'I've jammed it too,' he said. 'Keys won't work in it now, they'll have to break the door down to reach us.'

'Good,' I said.

'What are you doing?' Ketty asked.

'It's our only way out of here,' I said.

'What is?' Dylan snapped. 'You've just locked us *in*.'

'Where's Geri?' Ketty gasped.

'Trust me,' I said.

'But Geri …?' Dylan said.

'Geri's not helping,' Nico said, checking the door, as someone started thumping on the other side.

208

'Open up!' yelled a guard.

The door handle rattled, but the jammed lock held.

'What d'you mean, Geri's not helping?' Ketty asked.

'Get a second key,' another guard ordered from outside. 'This one's not working.'

'Quick,' I said. 'We have to—'

'No *way* Geri isn't helping,' Dylan said, folding her arms. 'What did she say?'

'There isn't time to explain,' Nico said. 'Do what Ed says.'

'But—'

'For once in your life, Dylan, just *listen*,' I shouted. 'We have to get out of this building and there's too much security just to walk out the front of the compound.'

Huge thumps now against the door. More yells. We had to hurry.

'In case you hadn't noticed,' Dylan said, narrowing her eyes, 'there's also too much security on the other side of this door to go through it. And there's no window in the room, so there *isn't* another way out.'

'Yes there is.' I looked from her to Ketty, meeting their eyes but easily resisting the pull to mind-read. 'It was something Djounsou said about the walls that made me realise. They're really thin, look, with spaces in-between to carry air ducts.' I stepped over to the wall opposite the door and gave it a sharp rap. It made a light, hollow sound. 'We use a battering ram to get through them. Find our way out of the compound through the spaces that run between the rooms.'

I saw them both register what I was saying, their eyes reflecting their view of the madness of this idea.

'I know it sounds crazy . . .' I said.

'. . . but at this point it's pretty much our only option,' Nico added.

Ketty glanced frantically round the empty room. 'Except there isn't anything we can use as a battering ram,' she said.

'Yes there is,' I said, as more thumps and yells rained down on the door.

'*What?*' Dylan glared at me.

'You,' I said.

23: ESCAPE

'*Me?*' Dylan blinked rapidly, her pale green eyes uncomprehending.

'Yes, *you*,' I said. 'The three of us ram you into the wall as hard as we can, and you use your Medusa ability to stop from getting hurt.'

The yells and thumps coming from the other side of the door had died down. Instead, the guards were muttering into walkie-talkies. I could hear the fuzz of the machines, though not what the men were saying.

'That is the most totally insane idea I've ever heard,' Dylan said, her eyes hardening.

My heart sank.

'But you'll give it a go?' Nico raised his eyebrows.

'I suppose so.' Dylan thought for a second, then turned her back on me and crossed her arms across her chest. 'Okay, Ed, I'm going to lean back on three. You take my shoulders. 1 – 2 – 3 . . .' She leaned back into my arms. I caught her and held her, as instructed. Nico reached for her thighs.

'Lower,' Dylan snapped. 'Nico, you hold just above the knee. Ketty can do higher up. *Jeez*, how come this never came up in our attack and defence lessons?'

Rolling his eyes, Nico took Dylan's legs and held her off the ground. Ketty ran over and grabbed Dylan round the hips. Between us, she was heavy, but manageable.

More muttering outside. I glanced up at the camera over the door. Anyone in the communications room would be able to see what we were doing – still, that couldn't be helped.

'Ready?' Nico said.

'Yup.' Dylan gritted her teeth.

'On my count,' Nico said. 'Ready ... steady ...'

I tightened my grip round Dylan's shoulders.

'Ram!'

The three of us charged towards the wall. *Wham.* The soles of Dylan's shoes made a dent in the plaster, nothing more.

'Take a bigger run-up,' she ordered.

We carried her back to the door. Outside we could hear the guards muttering to each other.

'There's something wrong with the lock,' one of them was saying. 'I'm going to try shooting it off.'

'Hurry up,' Ketty hissed.

Nico counted us down again.

Run. Ram. *Wham.*

A small hole appeared in the plaster.

'It's working,' Nico said, excitedly.

'Do it again,' Dylan said.

'You okay?' I asked her.

'Yeah,' she said, glancing up at me. 'Go on.'

3-2-1. *Wham.*

Dylan's feet broke through the wall.

A single gunshot on the other side of the door made us all jump.

Panic swamped my head. I stared at Nico.

'Keep going,' he shouted. 'I'll hold the door in place.' He frowned, focusing his gaze on the door.

It worked. The door stayed firmly shut, even as the guards hurled themselves against it.

We rammed Dylan's feet against the wall again – and again. I kept my focus on her face. She was clearly concentrating hard, her eyes squeezed tight shut. I couldn't tell from her expression if she was in any pain.

A couple more rams and there was a hole in the wall big enough to crawl through.

'That's it,' I said.

'Put me down.' Dylan shook herself as she stood up.

Ketty was already scrambling into the space behind the wall. 'There's just enough room to walk properly,' she called out. 'Come on.'

'Go right, then head left,' I said. 'There's a communications room near here. That's our best chance of finding the way out.'

I pushed Dylan in after Ketty. Nico was still concentrating on holding the door shut against the guards.

At that moment the shrieking alarm stopped. My ears

rushed with the sudden silence. I hurried after Dylan into the space behind the wall. The passageway was extremely narrow. Ketty, as the smallest of us, might have room to move about, but I could only just stand widthways.

I looked up. Ketty and Dylan were already out of sight in the gloom beyond. I raced after them, ducking my head to avoid the wires and pipes that ran along the inside of the wall. I could hear Nico right behind me, his breath heavy and ragged in my ear.

The roars of the guards echoed towards us. From the snatches I could pick up it was obvious that they were inside the wall but none of them were able to walk properly in the space and were having to stand sideways in order to move.

Good. That should buy us a little time.

I caught up with Dylan and Ketty. They'd stopped in front of a grille in the bottom of the wall. Light filtered through the wire mesh, casting a criss-cross pattern of shadows over our legs. Ketty crouched down, peered through the grille, then stood up again.

'This looks like the communications room,' she whispered. 'There's a big screen on the wall next to this grille and I can see security monitors on the wall opposite.'

'That's it,' I whispered.

Nico huddled closer. 'How many guards?' he asked.

'Just one,' Ketty whispered.

'Let me through.'

We shuffled along and Nico eased himself down beside the grille. In seconds he had telekinetically removed the screws holding the top two corners of the grille in place. I bent down and held the grille steady as he undid the bottom screws, then, between us, we took it out and laid it beside us.

Down the dark air duct corridor, the guards' footsteps were getting louder. Closer.

I peered into the communications room. The one security guard was busy studying the monitors on the wall opposite, his back turned to us.

'Hurry,' I whispered.

Nodding, Nico held up his hand. With a single twist he teleported the guard's gun out of his holster and rammed it, hard, against his head.

The guard fell to the floor with a thump.

'Nice work,' I murmured.

Nico grunted as he eased himself through the grille space. As the rest of us followed, Nico ran to the door that led back to the corridor where we'd been kept and telekinetically locked it. He gave his wrist an extra twist. 'There,' he said, 'jammed.'

'When did you work out how to do that?' I said.

'Under that frigging blindfold,' Nico muttered. 'I told you I've been practising.'

Ketty was at the other door, peering round.

'I can see the exit,' she said. 'Two guards on the inside.'

'There's another guard outside, by the exit to the compound.' I pointed at the security monitors.

Nico followed my gaze, staring intently at what we were up against. 'No problem,' he said.

215

'Come on, then.' Dylan ran over to Ketty at the door.

I glanced round. The big screen on the opposite wall caught my eye. It was an electronic whiteboard, loaded with a map. I went over. As I did, we could hear muffled shouts from the guards who'd been following us down the air duct passages.

They were almost here.

'Hurry, Ed,' Nico whispered.

I stared up at the map. The compound was clearly marked with a cross. A road ran past it. I scanned the map, searching for the name Mahore. *There.* It was one of a small cluster of villages to the north-east of the compound.

'Ed, what are you *doing*?'

I grabbed the electronic pen from the shelf below the whiteboard and ringed Mahore in a large black swirl.

Now Carson would know where to find us.

And I would be able to take my revenge for Luz.

Nico grabbed my arm and yanked me across the room. 'Frigging come on!' he snapped.

I joined the others, my heart pounding. We raced through the door, down carpeted floors – this part of the building was like a business office. The two guards on the front door turned as they heard us.

Before the men had time to reach for their guns, Nico had teleported them both into the air and slammed them against the glass wall behind. Then he turned and hurled them back out into the corridor behind.

Their yells rang out as they thumped onto the ground.

216

We raced through the front door, into bright, sudden light and stifling heat. I blinked in the glare of the sun.

'*Shit*.' Dylan pointed down the path. The guard at the exit point was watching us, his rifle raised to shoulder level.

'Stop. Now,' he barked.

Nico, Ketty and I skidded to a halt.

'For God's sake.' Dylan marched towards him, a look of grim determination on her face.

'Can she stop bullets?' I asked Ketty.

'I guess she thinks she can,' Ketty breathed, not taking her eyes off Dylan.

The guard was staring at her too, clearly bewildered by her lack of fear. His walkie-talkie crackled. He levelled his rifle at Dylan.

'Stop,' he ordered. 'Stop, or I'll shoot.'

I could hear the lie in his voice. 'He's been ordered to take us alive,' I said.

Shouts from inside the compound.

'He's not getting the chance to take us at all.' Nico darted sideways, as Dylan reached the guard.

She stopped just a metre in front of him. 'Go on, then,' she said defiantly. 'Freakin' shoot me.'

As she spoke, Nico twisted his hand and the rifle flew out of the guard's hand. It sailed into the distance. The guard reached for his handgun but Nico was too fast. He teleported the man flat onto his back, then shoved him away from us, in the opposite direction to the gun.

'They're outside!' It was Carson's voice.

I glanced up. He was racing into the carpeted entrance area, accompanied by the two guards Nico had sent flying earlier.

'Run!' I yelled.

The four of us pounded towards the exit. Gunfire behind us.

'Shoot the girls,' Carson shouted. 'Don't aim at the boys.'

'Charming,' Dylan muttered.

We raced onto the road beyond the exit. I glanced up and down the road. It was a dusty track – smooth, but not tarmac. No sign of any vehicles.

Nico peered round the wall back into the compound. 'Oh, man, Carson's got about ten guards with him.'

'I'll draw their fire,' Dylan shouted, lunging for the exit.

'No!' Nico yelled, but Dylan was already racing past him. A burst of gunfire.

'Oh God,' Ketty moaned. 'How are we going to get away?'

I looked up and down the road again. Was that a truck in the distance? Yes, it was roaring down the track towards us, dust billowing up from its wheels.

My heart leaped. 'We make the truck stop,' I said. 'I'll mind-read the driver.'

'How?' Ketty said. 'He won't be close enough.'

'I'll do it remotely.' I took a deep breath and focused on the driver. It was hard without seeing his face. I concentrated on telling him to stop as he reached us. *Get here and stop.* My head spun. I had no sense of connection with him.

218

'It's not working.' Ketty voiced my own desperate thoughts.

The truck was just a few metres away now. Rap music blared out from its window, mixing with the gunfire from the compound and Nico's yells as he continued to tell Dylan to get out of the way.

I closed my eyes. *Stop. Stop. Stop.*

'Noooo!' A high-pitched scream jerked my eyes open.

My whole body froze. Ketty was in the road. Arms out-stretched, pleading with the driver to stop.

But the truck wasn't slowing. I went to move, to push Ketty out of the way, but time slowed and my leg had barely left the ground before the truck was here. *Here.* Almost on top of her.

'Ke—!' My own yell had barely left my mouth when the truck screeched to a halt, just centimetres in front of Ketty.

She stood glassy-eyed, as the truck driver stuck his head out the window.

'What the hell you doing, stupid little bitch?' he shouted.

I raced round. He looked up. *Whoosh.* I was inside his mind. Ignoring all his panicky thoughts, I focused on pre-venting him from moving or speaking.

'Nico,' I yelled. 'We've got a ride!'

With a whoop, Nico was there. In a flash, he'd teleported the driver out of the truck and back down the road. Using the side of the truck as cover, he resumed his defence of us. The guards – and there were at *least* ten – were pouring out of the exit.

My heart raced. No way could Nico deal with all of them

219

on his own. For a moment it struck me that Nico and Dylan had been right about the attack and defence training we'd had back at school. We'd needed more of it, not less – so that Ketty and I could help too.

'Get in, Ed.' Dylan was dragging Ketty into the truck. Her eyes were still glazed over. What was wrong with her? A vision? Or had the truck hit her at the last minute without me realising? I scrambled into the driver's seat, feeling numb, as Dylan pushed Ketty into the passenger seat.

'Drive!' she yelled, hauling herself in next to Ketty.

'*What?*' I only knew about cars and stuff in theory. I'd never actually *driven* so much as a go-kart.

'Do it,' she ordered.

Between us, Ketty was groaning, coming to.

'Hurry up,' Nico's yell rose up from the back of the truck, barely audible above the gunfire. 'They're shooting at the tyres.'

There was no choice.

I turned the key, still in the ignition. The truck roared into life. I checked the gearstick and pushed it into first position. Then I pressed down on what I hoped was the clutch and the accelerator pedals. Dad had gone on about the clutch to me many times – how you had to use it to make the car change gear. *Yes.* It worked. The truck bucked and spluttered.

'Ease up on the freakin' gas,' Dylan shouted.

I lifted my foot off the accelerator a fraction and we sped away.

24: MAHORE

'Change gear!' Dylan yelled. She stuck her head out of the window and looked back at the compound.

I pressed down on the clutch again, then reached for the gearstick and wrenched it into the slot marked 2. The truck made a horrible, grinding sound, but – to my intense relief – kept going.

'You're driving?' Ketty said, weakly.

'Yeah.' I gripped the wheel and moved the gearstick into third position. 'How're we doing? Anyone following?' I glanced in the wing mirror, but all I could see was the dust our own wheels were throwing up behind.

'No ... wait, *yes*. They're turning out of the compound now. Two jeeps.' Dylan withdrew her head from outside the window. 'Step on the gas, will you?'

'You told me to ease up a few seconds ago.'

'This isn't a freakin' judgement on your driving,' Dylan shouted. 'We just need to go faster.'

'Stop yelling,' Ketty cut in. 'I feel sick.'

I glanced sideways at her. She did look very pale.

'I'll be fine,' she said, not looking round at me. 'I just had a horrible vision.'

'What of?'

'A fire ... it doesn't matter.'

'*Faster*, Ed,' Dylan urged.

I gritted my teeth, deployed the clutch and wrenched the gearstick into the slot marked 4. I pressed down on the gas pedal again. The truck zoomed forwards. I checked the speedometer on the dashboard. We were going at 60 miles an hour. I pressed harder on the accelerator and the dial rose to 70. Ahead I could see a crossroads. It wasn't mad busy, but there *were* other cars. I was going to have to stop, which meant right now I needed to be slowing down, not speeding up.

I took my foot off the gas and squinted into the fierce African sun, concentrating hard on the oncoming traffic. The road ahead shimmered with heat.

Dylan turned round, enraged. 'What the freakin' hell are you *doing*?' she shouted. 'Carson's men are, like, two metres behind us.'

'Okay, okay.' My heart was thumping fit to jump out of my chest. I pushed down on the accelerator again, forgetting to change gear. The truck bucked and rattled. The engine made a horrible grinding noise.

Beside me, Ketty sucked in her breath – a fearful gasp.

'*ED!*' Dylan swore.

'Don't stall, don't stall,' I muttered under my breath. Sweat was pouring off my forehead, my shirt sticking like a damp rag to my back.

The truck zoomed off again. The gunfire stopped.

'Have we lost them?' Ketty asked.

'No.' Dylan turned from the window. 'They're reloading.'

Oh, God.

'Is Nico okay?' Ketty asked.

'Fine,' Dylan said. 'He's trying to bang the two jeeps into each other. He's making them swerve, which is why they haven't shot out our tyres, but he can't make them crash.'

The crossroads up ahead was almost here. It suddenly seemed *full* of traffic. I was going to *have* to slow or I'd hit a car.

The gunfire started up again.

'Shit, that was close,' Dylan shrieked.

We passed a sign. Mahore was clearly signalled as a left-hand turn. I gripped the steering wheel. Up ahead the road was clear, just a lorry chuntering along in the distance. My heart leaped. I could slow a little and still make the turn before the lorry reached us.

'Careful, Ed,' Ketty warned. 'The traffic drives on the right.'

'Okay.' I focused on making my turn.

'Just get us onto that road,' Dylan yelled. '*Hurry!*'

I slowed the truck, ready to turn.

'They're right on top of us,' Dylan shrieked. 'They're aiming at Nico.'

'*No,*' Ketty gasped.

I looked left, at the oncoming traffic. *Oh God*, the lorry

223

was thundering along much faster than I'd realised. I hesitated a fatal second, unsure whether to wait for it to pass.

'TURN!' Dylan screamed.

I pushed down on the gas again and surged forwards. The lorry was right on top of us. I swung the wheel sharply. *Too* sharply. We spun into the road. Cars honked. The lorry was coming. I pressed the gas flat on the floor.

'Come *on*!' I roared.

Horn blaring, the lorry's brakes screeched behind us.

Smash!

I froze. But it wasn't us the lorry had hit.

'Yes!' Dylan was leaning right out of the window now, looking back, yelling out what she saw. 'Both jeeps rammed into that huge truck,' she said. 'I can see Carson. All the men. They're out of the jeeps. So's the truck driver. We've done it. We've got away!'

I nodded, my hands still clutching the steering wheel. Traffic was zooming towards us. Terrifying.

Ketty put her hand on my arm. 'You can slow down a bit now.'

I checked the speed dial. *Christ*, I was driving at eighty miles an hour. I gently released the gas pedal, feeling my body relax a little. The truck slowed to fifty miles an hour. There was still plenty of oncoming traffic, but the road straight ahead of me was clear.

After about twenty miles, there was another sign for Mahore. I waited for the traffic to clear completely, then took the left-hand turn. We travelled on, along another dusty, straight road for miles, but there were no more signs, despite a number of turnings.

The landscape around us looked like nothing I'd ever seen before. Unlike the desert in Spain, which had been full of bushy scrub and rocks, we were now surrounded by drifts of soft, yellow sand that spread out in all directions. There were no mountains on the horizon, just a few isolated trees, some shacks and houses in the distance and, beyond them, the huge, blue sky that met the land at right angles.

'Maybe we've missed the turning for Mahore,' I said uncertainly.

'We should stop over there and find out,' Dylan said as we approached a row of tin-roofed shacks.

'She's right,' Ketty said.

I nodded. Slowing, I pulled the truck over to the side of the road and pressed down on the brakes. The truck juddered to a halt. I bent over the steering wheel, suddenly completely exhausted.

'Come on,' Ketty said. 'Let's check on Nico, then find another ride.'

'Yeah, and when we get back in, *I'm* driving,' Dylan muttered.

Nico turned out to be fine but exhausted – and openly impressed by the way I'd swung the truck into the road just in front of the big lorry, not giving the jeeps following us time to slow down. I didn't tell him that the whole thing was really down to luck – and Dylan urging me to make the turn after I'd hesitated.

At least I hadn't crashed. Hopefully the truck would, at some point, find its way back to its owner. Remembering him reminded me of my failed attempt to mind-read him remotely. Why was it that the only people I seemed able to communicate with at a distance were the other people with the Medusa gene – and my sister? Well, there wasn't time to think about that now.

We wandered over to the row of tin-roofed shacks. In the speeding truck I hadn't realised how hot it was. Now we were outside and moving more slowly, the sun felt like a laser on the back of my neck.

One of the shacks had various stalls set up outside selling an array of produce, from rice to melons. Just inside the door I could see a pile of golden loaves and a row of water bottles.

My mouth watered at the sight of all the food. Nico saw me gazing hungrily at a tray of bananas. He glanced round, checking the coast was clear, then held up his hand. A thick bunch of ripe, yellow bananas zoomed into his palm. He walked on, whistling just a little self-consciously. I glanced at the stall. It seemed wrong to take food without paying for it – though I was absolutely starving and we had no money.

Ketty must have sensed my anxiety. Maybe she felt it too. Anyway, she whispered something to Dylan who rolled her eyes.

'You can't have my freakin' ring,' she said. 'But I guess I can spare this.' She slipped one of the silver bangles off her wrist and handed it to me. 'Go on, pay with that, Mr Ethics. You can ask for directions to Mahore at the same time.'

I smiled. At least Mr Ethics was an improvement on Chino Boy.

Dylan grinned back. 'That was a great move with the truck earlier, by the way, even though you and I both know that you choked before you turned.'

I rolled my eyes at her, then went inside the shack. A man in a wide straw hat was sitting on a stool by the counter, fanning himself. He looked up, lazily, as I came in. I offered him the bangle.

'We want some food,' I said, uncertain whether he would speak English. 'We took some bananas. We'd like some bread too. And water.'

The man frowned at the bangle, examining the hallmark and biting it a couple of times. In the end he shrugged. 'Okay,' he said.

I took two loaves of bread and a bottle of water each.

'Where you going?' the man said as I turned to leave.

'Mahore.' I pointed up the road. 'That way?'

The man nodded. 'I take delivery now. For another silver bracelet I take you?'

I nodded eagerly, then went outside to tell the others. Dylan agreed to hand over another bangle and we sat in the shade of the shack to eat the food while we waited for the shop owner.

The sun was fierce on our heads. My eyes stung from the glare and I could feel my skin burning. If Mum was here she'd have been nagging me about putting on suncream. Once she'd got over the fact that I'd just driven a truck and caused a car crash, that is.

Imagining Mum's outraged face almost made me smile.

'We should get to Mahore well ahead of Carson's men,' I said.

'Yeah, we should.' Nico raised his eyebrows. 'Their jeeps looked completely written off.'

'How was the lorry they smashed into?' I asked.

'Not a scratch, as far as I could see.' Nico laughed, then yawned. 'Jesus, I'm knackered.'

He leaned back against the wall and closed his eyes.

'Tell me again why we have to go to Mahore?' Dylan demanded.

I explained my promise to help Tsonga … to save his daughter. Thoughts of Luz filled my head as I spoke – of the promise I'd failed to keep to help her. I swallowed, trying to hold back the sob that threatened to rise up from my guts whenever I pictured her.

'But why isn't Geri helping?' Ketty asked.

I told her what Geri had said – how our priority was to get Carson and not get sidetracked by Djounsou's local ambitions to take over the region.

'But that's so wrong,' Ketty said, open-mouthed. 'They can't just stand by and ignore innocent people being massacred.'

'Oh, wake up,' Dylan snorted, flicking back her long red hair. 'Why *should* Geri and the government be interested in helping some poor little region in the middle of nowhere?

They don't have anything to give back – like money or oil –
do they? That's just how the world works.'

I sat back. I guessed Dylan was right. Not that it made any
difference.

'You don't have to come,' I said. 'Any of you.'

Dylan snorted again. 'Of course we're coming. Who cares
what Geri wants? Carson just does whatever he's paid to do.
Djounsou's the *main* villain.'

I gritted my teeth. 'No,' I said. 'We're getting Carson
too. That's why I left that ring round Mahore on the map
back in the compound – so he'll know where we are and
follow us.'

Ketty and Dylan both stared at me.

'And you did this because Djounsou and his army aren't
going to be enough of a challenge?' Dylan raised her eyebrows and glared at me. 'Couldn't we have left Carson alone
and just given Geri directions to his compound?'

I shrugged. That was what Geri had wanted, of course. But
as soon as Carson knew we were gone I was sure he'd dis-
appear too. Luring him to Mahore was the only way I could
be certain of getting revenge for what he'd done to Luz.

We sat for a few more minutes in silence. Nico fell asleep,
his head lolling against Ketty's shoulder. Then Dylan wandered away. Ketty glanced over at me and smiled.

'That vision earlier got me out of the block I was having,'
she said. 'I tried just now to see into our immediate future and
it worked.'

'What did you see?' I said.

229

'Us watching that fire,' she said. 'The one I saw in the earlier vision.'

I nodded, then focused on making contact with Amy again. I reached her mind easily enough and asked her to tell Geri we were going to Mahore and that Carson was following us there.

As I broke the connection, the shop owner appeared, car keys jangling from his hand. He said his name was Jimmy. We piled into his battered old Ford estate, squeezing ourselves in around a selection of crates – bananas and beans, mostly – and two dusty sacks of yams.

Thirty uncomfortable minutes later, we arrived at Mahore. There'd been no sign of Carson's men on the journey, though it was always possible they'd taken an alternative route.

'Very empty,' Jimmy said, peering out of the window at the deserted streets. 'I drop you here.'

My heart thudded. I checked my watch again. It was almost the time that Djounsou had said he would arrive. We got out of the car and headed towards the centre of town, where Jimmy said we would find St Luke's Church.

This was where Tsonga had said the weapons were hidden – where Djounsou had sent his men to round up Tsonga's brother and the other rebels.

A couple of minutes later, we reached the central square in Mahore. A crowd had gathered outside the church – a tall, imposing stone edifice in stark contrast to the rundown, crumbling houses that seemed to make up most of the rest of the town.

We walked closer, our eyes glued to the front of the church.

The large wooden door was open. A soldier was walking up and down beside it, clearly guarding the entrance.

Nico nudged one of the bystanders – a woman carrying a huge plastic bag. 'What's going on?' he said.

The woman shook her head. 'It is very bad,' she said. 'General Djounsou's soldiers have found weapons and men guarding them and they are threatening terrible things.'

'Where are the men?' I said.

The woman pointed at St Luke's. 'Inside there. Waiting for the general to arrive.'

We moved through the crowd, trying to get a better view without exposing ourselves to the door guard. A series of wide stone steps led up to the church door. Several hundred people were milling on the steps and in the square beyond, muttering to each other about what Djounsou would do when he arrived. The tension in the air made the heat even heavier.

We passed the steps and peered down the side of the church. A wooden door was set into the wall. Further down, towards the end of the church, was a series of stained glass windows. Beside me, Ketty gasped. 'Oh, no,' she said.

'What?' Nico and I spoke at once.

'This is the place from my visions.' Ketty's eyes were wide as she stared up at the stained glass window on the church wall. 'This is where I saw the fire.'

25: MAHORE

Before I had time to register what Ketty had said, a car horn blared out. We whipped round to see Djounsou arriving in an open-topped jeep. He was dressed in full khaki uniform and accompanied by six armed guards. We ducked behind a wall, keeping ourselves hidden as he strode up the church steps. Flanked by two soldiers with rifles, Djounsou faced the crowd.

A few people called out names: 'Thug ...' 'Butcher ...' but Djounsou just stood there, solid and unmoved, shaking his head.

'I am a father to Mahore,' he shouted. 'Like a father, I want what is best for the people. Like a father, I offer you protection. Like a father, I am misunderstood when I try to help ...'

More catcalls. I waited, my heart racing.

'I come here as a father, to bring you the security you crave. But a father has to be strong. A father has to be brave. Some of you have plotted against me. Rebellious children, fighting against your father.' He paused. 'Those people must be punished.'

Djounsou gave a signal and Tsonga appeared from the jeep. One of Djounsou's soldiers pushed him roughly onto the church steps. The crowd gasped as it caught sight of Tsonga's bruised and bloodied face. One eye was completely swollen shut and there was a long, purple gash across his cheek. His hands were tied behind him with a length of rope.

'How many men do you think we could handle between us?' Nico whispered.

I clutched the wall we were hiding behind. Despite the hot sun just a metre away, the shadowed stone felt cool under my hand.

'Not enough,' I whispered back. 'Not against soldiers with guns.'

Another signal from Djounsou and five more people were brought out from inside the church. Three of them were men. One of them had the same high forehead and stubborn expression as Tsonga – his brother, presumably. Next to him stood a woman dressed in a blue dress. She was shaking. A small girl held her hand. As soon as the little girl caught sight of Tsonga she tried to dart towards him, but the woman pulled her back.

'That must be Tsonga's brother and his wife,' Ketty whispered.

'And the little girl must be Tsonga's daughter, Victoria,' I said.

'Sssh,' Dylan hissed. 'Listen.'

Djounsou was talking again, about loyalty and dis-obedience.

'These people have betrayed me,' he said. 'Betrayed all of us. Betrayed our family.'

No. That's not right. An angry murmur ran through the crowd, yet no one called out.

'They're scared,' Ketty whispered in my ear. 'There are too many soldiers for us to fight against.'

I nodded, my heart sinking. *Too many soldiers for Nico to disable alone. Too many potential threats for Dylan to protect herself from. Too many minds for me to hold all at once.*

'Bring me the weapons,' Djounsou ordered.

As if they'd been waiting for the cue, three soldiers appeared from inside the church. Each one carried a large crate overflowing with guns and ammunition. A fourth soldier pointed his gun at the crowd, which parted, clearing a path to Djounsou's jeep. The soldiers started loading the weapons into the back.

Djounsou drew himself up, waiting until the angry muttering in the crowd subsided. Then he took his gun and held it at Tsonga's brother's head.

'These rebels must be punished.' He paused. 'Take them inside the church and tie them up.'

Tsonga glanced at his brother – a terrible look of loyalty and pain. Then the soldiers shoved the brother, his wife and the other two rebels through the church door. Djounsou, Tsonga and little Victoria were left outside.

Ketty gripped my arm. 'Maybe he won't hurt Tsonga's daughter?'

I shook my head. What was Djounsou playing at? The little girl was shaking now, standing at the top of the steps. Her lips trembled as she looked over at her father. He smiled encouragingly, but even from where we were standing you could see the fear in his eyes.

'We live in hard times,' Djounsou said, 'and no father wants to see his children suffer. But wicked actions must be punished. My soldiers have children too. *I* am a good father.' He pointed at Tsonga. 'This man is not. He has sacrificed his own daughter to a false ideal.' Djounsou's gaze swept across the crowd – angry, imperious, demanding. I shrank back into the shadows.

My mind spun. I couldn't see how we could save *anyone*. The odds were just too heavily stacked against us.

'And so the sins of the father are visited upon the sons,' Djounsou said slowly. 'Or, in this case, the daughter.' He turned to another soldier. 'Take her inside the church too. Tie her to the cross.'

'No, please, *no*.' Tsonga pleaded.

'Daddy!'

My guts clenched as little Victoria was dragged away.

Another signal from Djounsou and one of the soldiers from the jeep appeared with a metal can. He disappeared inside the church. A few moments later he was back, walking backwards out of the church, splashing the liquid from the can in front of him. He finished at the church door and turned,

235

swinging the empty can so that the final few drops spattered across the crowd.

I caught the smell immediately. Petrol.

'He's going to set fire to the church,' Nico breathed.

I caught Ketty's eye. *This* was her vision.

'He's going to burn all the rebels to death.' Dylan sucked in her breath. 'Even that little girl. That's totally *evil*.'

I couldn't believe what Djounsou was doing. And yet, it made sense. By killing Victoria and the others, Djounsou would personally punish Tsonga *and* send a message to Mahore and beyond not to mess with him.

'We can't let him do this,' I said, as Djounsou produced a lighter from his pocket.

'What can we do?' Ketty wailed. 'I mean, Nico could teleport that lighter out of Djounsou's fingers ...'

'... but there'll always be another lighter ...' Dylan finished, grimly.

The crowd, whose voices had risen again at the sight and smell of the petrol, quietened as Djounsou held the lighter right in Tsonga's face.

'This is your punishment for fighting me,' Djounsou said, calmly. 'You will watch your daughter die – before I kill you.'

'NOOO!' Tsonga's roar brought the crowd to life. They jeered, surging forwards, as he kicked and struggled against the soldiers holding him.

I gripped the wall in front of me more tightly. Maybe the crowd could stop Djounsou.

But Djounsou simply signalled one of his soldiers to fire.

The gunshot blasted into the air and a shocked silence fell again. Tsonga stood, defeated, his chest heaving as Djounsou flicked the lighter on and tossed the flame behind him, into the petrol that streaked around the church door.

Fire rose up immediately, licking at the door.

'Oh my God,' Ketty moaned beside me.

The crowd fell into a shocked silence. My heart seemed to stop beating.

Think of something. I had to get inside the church. Somehow I had rescue Victoria and the others. But how?

'What do we do?' Nico's forehead was furrowed with a deep frown. 'Telekinesis won't work against a fire.'

'No,' I said, 'but it will work against locked doors. Come with me. If you can get me through that side door we saw, I can try and rescue the people inside.'

'You can't do that,' Nico said, horrified.

'Just get me inside.' I raced off. As I ran I glanced at Djounsou and his men up on the church steps. They were facing the blazing door Djounsou had just set alight, not looking into the hushed crowd. I kept my head down anyway, keeping close to the far wall as I ran.

As I reached the side of the church, the others caught up with me.

'You can't go in there, Ed,' Ketty panted. 'It's too dangerous.'

'She's right, the fire's too big,' Dylan added. 'And even if I could get past the flames, none of us would survive the smoke. The people inside have only got a couple of minutes as it is.'

237

I turned to Nico. 'Just open the door for me.'

'No,' he insisted. 'It'd be suicide.'

I stared at him. Somewhere in my head I knew he was trying to help me, but right then all I could feel was fury. 'Then I'm going in the front,' I snapped.

I turned away.

'You can't,' Ketty shrieked. She grabbed my arm. 'Nico, stop him.'

'Ed, man, *please*.'

'You can't just stroll over and walk in through that main door,' Dylan added. 'If Djounsou doesn't kill you, the fire will.'

I turned back, facing the three of them. I took in the tension on their faces. The fear. And suddenly my anger at them vanished. They just didn't understand.

To Nico, Dylan and Ketty, the death of the rebels – and Luz – was a terrible tragedy that didn't, in the end, have anything to do with them. Just as Geri and the government thought that it didn't have anything to do with them, either.

It wasn't like that for me.

I have to go,' I said, simply. 'I promised Luz I'd help her. And I got everything wrong and she died. Then I promised Tsonga I'd help save his daughter. I have to try.'

'But you might die,' Ketty said.

I shrugged. 'I can't live with myself if I don't at least try. Not after I promised to help ...'

The others all stared at me, then Nico spoke.

238

'You've got two minutes to get in and out, then I'm coming in after you and if that happens I'll die too, so you'll be killing me as well, okay?'

'Fine,' I said. 'Just open the door.'

'I already did.'

I raced down the side of the church. As I ran I tore a strip off my shirt and wound it quickly round my mouth. I reached the side door and hurled myself at the handle.

Inside the church I stood for a second, letting my eyes get used to the darkness. I was in a small room of some kind. I could smell smoke in the distance. A grey wisp curled under the door in front of me. I pushed it open.

Oh God.

Smoke rose up from a pathway of flames that led from the main door, all the way down the aisle, to the wooden altar where Tsonga's brother and the other adults were tied to the legs. One of the men was slumped, unconscious, the others were shouting for help.

None of them noticed me. My stomach twisted as I looked round for Victoria. *There.* Almost hidden from view behind the altar, she was sitting down, tied with rope to the gold cross that towered up in front of the stained glass windows at the far end of the church.

She was coughing from the smoke – and crying. A shaft of sunlight fell across her black hair, lighting the wispy curls at the front.

My heart beat fast. The smoke was already almost suffocating. There was no way I was going to be able to save all

239

five of them. My stomach cramped with fear. I took a huge breath, ready to run to the altar.

And then a hand grabbed my arm. I spun round, ready to fight.

It was Nico. Dylan and Ketty stood on either side of him looking grimly determined. *No.* They weren't going to stop me. Didn't they understand I *had* to do this? I ripped the scrap of cloth off my mouth.

'I told you I—'

'Don't freak out, Mr Ethics,' Dylan snarled.

'We do this together,' Nico said firmly.

'Or not at all,' Ketty added.

I blinked, huge waves of emotion flooding through me. Shock at their decision, mixed with honour at their loyalty and terror that now more lives were at stake.

I took another deep breath, as fresh hope surged through me. Maybe now there was a chance to save everybody.

'Come on, then,' I said. 'Let's go.'

26: FIRE

We raced down the side aisle. Victoria's screams filled my head. I made straight for her, trying to ignore the smoke that filled my lungs, burning my chest. Coughing, I reached the little girl and slid to my knees, feeling for the knots that tied her to the cross.

I couldn't get a hold of the rope properly. Victoria was thrashing about, completely hysterical, eyes tight shut, kicking out with her legs. I glanced over my shoulder. I needed Nico's help with the knots, but he was on the other side of the altar, busy telekinetically untying the adults' ropes.

'Nico!' I called, choking in the foul air.

'In a sec,' he yelled, not looking round. Dylan was beside him, stamping her hands and feet at the flames threatening the rebels.

'It's okay, Victoria, I'm going to help you,' I shouted, feeling my own panic rising.

'Daaa-deee!' she cried.

241

Ketty touched my shoulder. 'I'll deal with the rope,' she said. 'You calm her down.'

I nodded. 'Victoria, look at me.'

The little girl didn't even hear me. I grabbed her chin and forced her round. Her eyes shot open, wild and staring.

Whoosh. I'd never felt such naked terror before. Victoria's mind was a chaos of panic – *can't breathe, can't breathe*, was the only coherent thought in her head.

Listen to me, Victoria. We're going to help you. Hold still so we can get your ropes off. Then we'll take you to Daddy.

I could feel Victoria's mind latch onto mine. She didn't question the fact that I was inside her head, or even who I was.

Keep still, I urged again.

Victoria stopped struggling. I broke the connection. Ketty was fumbling with the knot that tied Victoria to the cross. She was coughing badly. I glanced round. Nico was still with the adults. Two of the men were up now and racing down the side aisle, dragging Tsonga's sister-in-law between them. She was clearly unconscious, her head slumped awkwardly to one side.

Tsonga's brother lay on the ground. Nico stood over him. He looked at Dylan and shook his head. Dylan turned away, bent over, coughing like her lungs would explode.

My heart sank. Tsonga's brother was dead. This little girl at my feet was all Tsonga had left. I *had* to rescue her.

'Nico,' I yelled.

He turned and held his hand up. With a twist the rope tying

Victoria to the cross sprang free. On the other side of the altar table, Dylan slid to the ground. I jumped to my feet.

'Dylan!' I yelled.

She was out cold. Nico hauled her up with a mix of telekinesis and brute strength. He slung her over his shoulder and yelled at Ketty.

'Bring the little girl,' Nico shouted. '*Now!* Let's go.'

He sped off, Dylan bumping against his back. I turned back to Ketty and Victoria.

'Come on,' I yelled.

Ketty looked past me to the door. She grabbed my arm. 'Ed!'

I spun round, just in time to see Nico and Dylan disappearing behind a wall of flame. For a second I couldn't make sense of what I was looking at, then I realised. The fire had brought down the archway that led out to the side door of the church. Nico and Dylan had just got through, before the collapse.

And now the fire was too big for us to pass. There was no way out.

'Oh, God, oh my God.' Ketty was shouting and choking and crying all at once.

I glanced round, my heart pounding. The side door and the main door were consumed with flames. What other exit could there be? Victoria's hand crept into mine. She was doubled over, coughing. I reckoned we had about twenty seconds left of the two minutes Dylan had predicted we would last.

I looked at Ketty. Tears were streaming down her face. She met my gaze.

Whoosh.

I'm so sorry, Ketty. So sorry …

This can't be it, she thought-spoke.

I'm so sorry. I didn't know what else to say. Beside me, I felt Victoria clutch at my shirt, burying her mouth against the cloth to try and keep out the smoke. I was coughing like my lungs were turning inside out. My head felt light. It was impossible to think. Ketty was gabbling thought-speech inside my head. I could barely hear her for the thunder of my own thoughts, my own fear.

It was over. The fire had got us.

And then Ketty's words broke through. *Ed,* listen*, I mean it, this* can't *be it. In my vision I saw the side of the church on fire, properly on fire with flames and everything.*

So?

Well, I had to be outside to see that, didn't I? Which means I'm going to make it outside, which means you are too.

I broke the connection, filled with fresh hope. If we couldn't go forwards, maybe there was a way out behind us.

Yes. Behind the altar, to the right, was a small wooden door.

I turned, dragging Victoria with me. Ketty ran alongside, her hand over her mouth.

We tore through the door into some sort of wood-panelled office. A table stood against one wall. Above it was a shelf covered in bowls and boxes. Robes hung from a row of pegs on the wall. I looked desperately round.

'Here.' Ketty raced across the room to a tiny wooden door

244

set into the panelling. She flung it open. It led straight onto a narrow flight of stairs.

'Victoria.' I bent down to her level. She'd stopped coughing quite so furiously now and was staring at me with huge brown eyes.

'Where do those stairs go?'

'Up.' She frowned. 'Are you an angel?' she said.

I blinked. 'Er ... no,' I said.

'Come on.' Ketty raced up the stairs.

Coughing, I followed, clutching Victoria's hand.

The stairs were narrow and twisty, but the air was a little clearer here. I took a breath, clearing my head a little, as we reached the top of the stairs.

'Where now?' Ketty looked round, frantically searching for another door.

'Over there.'

I followed Victoria's pointing finger to a small door set into the far wall. I reached up and slid back the bolts, then pushed Victoria through.

'Where does this lead?' Ketty asked.

'To the bells,' Victoria said.

Of course ... a bell tower. Maybe there'd be a way out through here onto the roof. I helped Ketty scramble through after Victoria, then hauled myself up. As I pulled myself through the opening, I glanced back down the twisty little staircase. Smoke was already pouring up after us. A finger of flame curled round the doorway.

God, how could it spread that fast?

I wriggled inside the bell tower, then slammed the door shut behind me. The tower was tall, but narrow. Three bells hung high above our heads from the centre of the peaked ceiling. Their ropes dangled in the small space. Ketty and Victoria were crouched opposite me, beside an empty crate. Victoria was sobbing for her dad, Ketty stroking her hair.

I looked round, my heart sinking. There was no door ... no window ... no way out. Wait, there *must* be. There was enough light in the room to see the others quite clearly – where was it coming from? I turned round and stood up. There, above my head, was a tiny, shuttered window. Sunshine filtered through its slats, casting a series of shadowy stripes across the wooden floor. A fly buzzed past my head. For a second I felt the dampness of my shirt against my back and the soreness of my eyes from the smoke. I stood on tiptoe, opened the window and flung the shutters wide. Light flooded the room.

'YES!' Ketty yelled. 'Come on!'

Victoria rubbed her eyes as I grabbed the crate beside them, turned it over and stood on it. From here I could see out through the window. Flames from the other end of the church were already licking towards us, twisting up into the bright blue sky above. Just below the window was a narrow ledge. Barely enough room for one of us to balance on. And then how did we get down? We were at the very top of the church here. Any attempt to jump would kill us.

The cries of the people at the front of the church wafted up towards me but I could only see the street at the side of the church from here. It was deserted – everyone must still be at the front.

'Can we get down from here?' Ketty asked from inside the bell tower.

'Sure,' I said. *Please, God, let that be true.*

'Can you see the others?' she asked.

I searched for a flash of Dylan's red hair. There was no sign of her, and yet she and Nico must be down there somewhere, mustn't they?

A new panic grabbed me round the throat. Suppose they *hadn't* got through the fire in time? I tried to picture Nico's face.

Nico! Nico!

Whoosh.

Frigging hell, Ed, man, are you okay?

Thank God.

Yes, we're on top of the church roof, in the bell tower. There's a window but you can only see it from the side.

We're coming.

I broke the connection. Seconds later, Nico and Dylan appeared in the street to the side of the church. They were looking up, their hands shielding their eyes from the sun.

I waved my arms frantically and focused on Nico's face again, struggling to keep my breath steady enough to picture him in my mind's eye.

There.

Can you see us? I thought-spoke.

247

Yeah. Hold on, I'll teleport you down.

Wait. Let me get the others.

No. One at a time. I can't handle more.

Okay, Victoria first.

I drew back, into the bell tower. Ketty and Victoria stared anxiously up at me.

'Come on.' I hauled Victoria up and balanced her on the window ledge.

'Ed, there's smoke coming in,' Ketty said, her voice tight with fear.

'No ... no ... too high ...' Victoria was struggling against me, trying to get back inside the bell tower.

I focused on Nico again.

Can you see her? I thought-spoke.

Yes. Let her go. I've got her.

I broke the connection, then turned to the little girl.

She was shaking, crying, clutching my hand. With a jolt I realised she had wet herself. I took a deep breath.

'Listen, Victoria, you have to be really brave now. When I said I wasn't an angel, I lied. I am. And I'm going to let go of you now and another angel's going to float you down to the ground, back to your dad.'

Victoria stopped struggling for a second, her mouth wide open with shock. At that moment I felt the tug of Nico's telekinesis pulling her away. I let go. Victoria screamed, then toppled off the roof.

I watched as she fell, my heart in my mouth ... one metre ... two ... All of a sudden her fall halted. Nico had her. She floated in mid-air, arms flailing, then carried on descending.

I drew back into the bell tower again. It was full of smoke now. Ketty's breath was coming in hoarse gasps. 'Help me get up there,' she said, her eyes streaming from the smoke.

I reached out, grabbed her under the armpits and hauled her up, onto the window ledge. Panting, I caught sight of the flames from the front of the church. They were snaking, fast, across the roof towards us.

Victoria was almost on the ground now. I waited until she was down, then leaped into Nico's mind again.

Ketty's ready, I thought-spoke. *Take her next.*

Sure, listen, Ed, Geri's here. Dylan just saw her. She's got Djounsou. She was yelling at him to tell her where we were.

So Tsonga's safe?

Yeah. Let me take Ketty.

I broke the connection. 'Nico's going to teleport you down,' I said.

Ketty glanced back at the smoke-filled tower room. Then across the roof, where the flames were devouring the space between us.

'Hold on to me,' she said. 'Nico can take us both.'

She grabbed my hand. I felt the tug of Nico's telekinesis, pulling her away.

'No, it's too hard for him. He has to take us one at a time.'

Ketty glanced across at the fire. The flames were inches away now, their heat fiercer than the sun's. '*Ed.*'

The telekinetic force pulling her away from me grew stronger.

'Go.' I wrenched my hand away.

With a yell, Ketty soared away from me, over the edge of the roof.

The flames licked at the corner of the window ledge. Smoke was pouring up from the whole building. I could no longer see Ketty, or the ground below.

Hurry up, Nico, hurry.

I balanced myself on the window ledge, one hand holding on to the frame. In the distance I could hear the whirr of a helicopter overhead but all my focus was on Nico. I made myself resist the urge to break into his mind again. He knew I was up here. As soon as Ketty was down he'd get me.

Except ... if I couldn't see him, then he wouldn't be able to see me ... My guts twisted. He'd be able to imagine it, wouldn't he? He'd seen where the others were. It would be okay.

CRASH! There was a terrible smashing and creaking and the roof in front of me collapsed. Through the smoke I could see down to the church beneath. The window ledge juddered and shifted.

'Oh God, Nico, hurry ...' I held my breath, waiting for the tug of his telekinesis. Surely Ketty must be down now?

Unless ... I could hardly bring myself to think it ... unless the roof caving in had somehow sent debris flying onto Nico ... or Ketty herself ...

Above me, the roar of a helicopter filled the air. I

glanced up. The machine was hovering above the roof, a rope ladder dangling from its open door. My heart leaped as fire curled round my feet.

It must be Geri. Nico had said she was here. She'd sent the helicopter to rescue me. I tried to still my mind enough to communicate with Nico, but I was in too much of a state to focus, my whole attention on the helicopter above. The rope ladder was almost touching the roof now, flames licking at the bottom rung.

'ED!' A man in a green jumper was leaning out of the helicopter, yelling down at me. 'Geri's here. Come on! Grab the rope.' I lunged for it. Missed. Almost fell. I gasped as the rope ladder swung back. I grabbed again. Contact. I hurled myself at the rungs. Scrabbled for a footing. Shut my eyes. *Yes.*

I held on tight, feeling the swoop and sway of the helicopter taking me up high into the clean, clear air. My stomach lurched with nausea.

'ED!' The man was shouting again, but I could only just make out the words as the wind whipped past my face.

I opened my eyes. We were high above Mahore. Fear froze me as I looked down.

'Ed, climb up.'

He had to be kidding. I closed my eyes tight shut and gripped the rope ladder.

'It's safer inside. Come on, there's no breeze. The helicopter is holding steady for you.'

I opened one eye.

251

'It's just four more rungs. Come *on*.'

I hesitated another second. The man was right, it would be safer inside.

'Come on, I'll be able to reach you if you just come up a couple more rungs.'

Staring straight ahead of me, and fighting the fear and nausea that was gripping me, I slid one hand, then the next, up the rope ladder.

The rungs moved gently in the still air. 'It's okay,' I muttered to myself. 'You can do this.' Holding on tight with my hands, I moved first one foot then the other onto the next rung up.

'You're doing great,' the man shouted. 'Keep coming, I've almost got you.'

I slid my hands up the rope ladder again. Clung on. Then moved my feet, one after the other. I was almost at the helicopter now. Another person had joined the first man, their knees appearing at the door just above my head.

The second person reached down and grabbed my arm. And then I looked up – and almost lost my grip entirely.

I was staring into a face I knew – but it wasn't Geri's.

Just above me, his hand gripping my arm, his eyes covered with mirrored sunglasses, was Blake Carson.

27: THE FALL

Carson's mouth stretched into a smile at the sight of my shocked face.

'Good to see you, kiddo,' he shouted over the roar of the helicopter engine. 'Now get on board.'

He grabbed me tightly by both arms and tried to haul me towards him. I clung to the rope ladder, which swung violently.

'No!' I yelled. I glanced down. *Oh God, oh God.* Mahore was so far below us now the people and cars looked like toys.

The sight made me giddy.

'Come on!' Carson's fingers dug into my arm like pincers.

I tried to pull away and my right foot slipped off the rope ladder. Panicking, I swung wildly, desperate to bring it back into position. My left foot slipped too. I dropped down, hanging from my hands as the rope ladder jerked and bucked in the air. Carson had slid forwards till half his chest was hanging over the open helicopter door. Fear choked me.

'ED!' Carson's voice was desperate. 'Get your feet back on the ladder.'

I closed my eyes. Please let him be there.

Whoosh.

Nico?

I'm here. I can see you. And that bastard. His thought-speech was calm. Determined. *I'm ready.*

I looked up into Carson's face, at his mouth, open in horror.

'Let go!' I shouted.

'No way!' he yelled back, gripping my arms even tighter.

The man beside him pulled out a gun.

'Let go!' I repeated.

'No.' I could feel Carson's hold on my arms slipping. I took a deep breath and took both hands off the rope ladder.

Now Carson was carrying all my weight. The muscles in his arms bulged as he held on to me.

'Let go of me,' I shouted again. 'Or you'll fall too.'

'No.' Carson shook his head, but his grip was slackening. He couldn't hold me. My arms slid through his hands, dragging him forwards. He was almost out of the helicopter now, the man beside him panicking, grabbing at his legs.

And then it happened. With a yell, Carson tipped forward, and fell completely out of the helicopter, still gripping my arms.

His sunglasses dropped away as we spun towards the ground.

Falling. Wind rushing past. Panic rising up. For a split

254

second that felt like a lifetime our eyes met. Inside Carson's mind I saw a mirror image of the pure terror that was gripping me.

And then he let go of my arms. My mouth opened in a silent scream. But before I could call out, I felt Nico's telekinesis tug at my body.

My fall stopped. For a moment I was held, suspended, in the bright African sky. I stared down at Carson, spinning away beneath me. His thin scream pierced my ears. I watched, unable to tear my eyes from him as he plunged down ... down ...

Down. The thin scream stopped. I looked, trying to make sense of what I saw – his body, twisted, on the ground beside the church.

Dead. He was dead.

My brain tried to process it, but my heart was racing. I was falling again. The sky was speeding past and yet I felt like I was sinking in slow motion. My head whirled. Seconds passed that felt like minutes. I just had time to register that I wasn't near the church any more and then I landed with a bump on the dusty earth.

I flopped back, winded. A moment later I felt the telekinesis release me. I relaxed into the solid ground beneath me and closed my eyes.

Footsteps in the distance, rushing closer ... around me. I wanted to open my eyes, but it was too big an effort.

'Is he okay?' Ketty said, breathlessly. I could feel her thudding to the ground beside me.

'Yes.' That was Nico. He paused, then said with less conviction, 'at least he *should* be.'

'Look, Daddy, it's the angel,' Victoria squealed.

I forced open my eyes. The little girl's face was inches above mine, filling my whole field of vision. Her eyelashes fluttered as she blinked, excitedly.

'Hi,' I croaked.

'He's okay,' Ketty said, her voice halfway between a sob and a cheer.

'He's saying hello,' Victoria announced. 'The angel.'

'Stop talking nonsense, Victoria, he is a brave boy who fell, not an angel,' Tsonga said, his deep, tender voice such a strong contrast to her high-pitched squeak that I smiled.

'But, Daddy, he *said* he was.'

'Get back, Victoria, let the man breathe.'

Somewhere above me a phone rang. I could hear Ketty answering it, her voice fading as she walked away.

'Bye, angel,' Victoria whispered. Her face vanished. I lay still, staring up at the clear blue sky above me. There was silence for a second. Then Nico's face came into view.

'*Angel?*' He grinned.

'Piss off,' I said. 'Er ... and thanks for getting me down.'

Nico affected a modest smile. 'No sweat, man. Last few seconds I couldn't see you so I had to sort of half-guess/half-sense when you were down.'

I struggled onto my elbows and looked round. I was lying in the middle of a dirt track. Roughly ploughed fields led off in all directions.

256

'Mahore's behind you,' Nico said. 'You landed on the outskirts.'

I twisted round. Just a couple of metres away, the dirt track I was on ended in a row of simple wooden houses, which led to more roads. The church was visible a few streets away – a burning tower of flame and smoke rising above the town.

Tsonga reached over and shook my hand. 'Thank you,' he said. 'The others told me how brave you were, going into St Luke's to save Victoria. I can never repay you.'

I blushed, not knowing what to say. 'I'm sorry about your brother.'

Tsonga nodded, his battered face heavy with sadness.

'I take Victoria away now,' he said. 'Somewhere where we will both be safe.'

The little girl waved and they walked off, back into Mahore. Nico stood next to me, watching them go.

'Will they be okay in there?' I said. 'What about Djounsou?'

'Geri's dealing with him,' Nico said.

Ketty walked back towards us. 'That was Geri on the phone. She's coming right over.'

I closed my eyes again. I was glad Carson and Djounsou had been stopped. And yet, knowing that they were out of the picture and that Victoria and Tsonga were safe didn't seem to change anything.

Luz was still dead. I was still responsible for that.

A moment later and Geri appeared, racing up the dirt track towards us. My mouth gaped as I saw her. Her normally neat blonde bob was all messy and there were dark stains all over her jacket. She was accompanied by two agents in jeans and dark glasses, and held a gun in her hand. Dylan was following a few paces behind.

'Are you all right, Ed?' Geri asked.

'I'm fine. Er, what's happening to Djounsou?'

'We've disarmed him and sent him and his soldiers packing. Once I'd spoken to Nico and Dylan, I realised taking them into custody wouldn't get you out of that church, so we focused on the job in hand.'

I stared at her. Was that, still, really all she cared about?

'But Djounsou will be back,' I said. 'Tsonga might have time to get his daughter somewhere safe, but it doesn't alter the fact that Djounsou's trying to take over the region and—'

'There's nothing we can do about that, Ed,' Geri said firmly. 'Like I told you, it's not our problem.'

I shook my head. Could none of them see that it was, absolutely, our problem? That cruelty and violence were *everyone's* problem?

Nico cleared his throat. 'Geri was all set to send men in after you. That's when you made contact with me. I was concentrating so hard I didn't even notice Carson's helicopter until the church roof collapsed.'

'I'd only just got down,' Ketty explained. 'Nico was running to get me out of the flames, that's why he didn't bring you down straight away.'

I nodded, all the pieces fitting together.

*

258

Two hours, and another vomit-making helicopter ride later, we were rested and bathed and sitting in the girls' hotel room in some big African city I can't remember the name of.

The others were in high spirits. Geri had promised that we didn't have to attend any more camps and she was planning on sending us back to Britain, to a secret location, for some rest and relaxation. 'Your families will be allowed to visit and, from now on, I shall be involved in your lives on a day-to-day level, overseeing both your training programme and your Medusa Project activities.'

The others couldn't see further than the promise of family visits. But I couldn't face being part of the project any more.

Not the way Geri ran it.

Behind me, the others were lounging on the beds, laughing.

'No way,' Nico teased Ketty. 'If we were in Scooby Doo then you'd be Shaggy.'

'If I'm Shaggy, then you're Fred.' Ketty laughed. 'Totally vain and not quite as clever as you think you are.'

'*What?*' Nico turned to her in mock-horror.

'*I'm* Fred.' Dylan wrinkled her nose. 'And by the way, Fred's not vain or stupid. He's the leader. The smart one.'

'But Velma's the one who always figures stuff out. She's the *really* smart one,' Ketty argued.

'Then Ed would be Velma,' Dylan said. '*I'm* Fred.'

I looked round. What were they all going on about?

'You okay?' Ketty smiled, but I could see the anxiety in her eyes. She was worried about me.

I nodded. 'Listen—'

259

But before I could say what I needed to, the door opened and Geri walked in. She looked like she had the first time I'd met her, smartly dressed in a red suit with not a single hair spoiling the sleek line of her bob.

'The flights are booked,' she announced. 'We leave first thing in the morning. You'll have a week to recover, then a week of intensive training, then it's back to missions. We're going to have to use more cunning to get you in play than we did before. But this experience should give you a lot of confidence. Now I know you'll be able to handle whatever I throw at you.'

I looked round at the others. Weren't they going to object to being used like this? A sullen silence met Geri's words. Nobody spoke.

'You'll be pleased to hear that Fernandez and the local police are under investigation and the street children you rescued from that cellar in San Juan are being looked after by the proper Spanish authorities.' She sighed. 'I owe you all an apology for sending you to that training camp.'

'We shouldn't have been sent to *any* kind of camp,' Dylan said.

'Maybe not, dear.' Geri paused. 'But you can't deny that you needed a lesson in discipline ... because what you did before ...'

'Because what we did before was *right*.' The words were out of my mouth before I'd realised I was going to speak. Everyone stared at me. 'And we're going to carry on doing just that. The right thing. At least, I am.'

Geri frowned. I met her eyes, resisting the pull to mind-read

260

her. We stared at each other and, for the first time, I realised how small-minded and uptight she really was.

'I'm not trying to stop you doing the right thing,' she said briskly. 'All the criminals I'm going to send you after need to be stopped.'

I shrugged. 'Maybe. That isn't the point.'

Geri cleared her throat. I could feel Nico, Dylan and Ketty watching me, but I kept my eyes on Geri.

'Ed,' she said in a conciliatory tone, 'I know you've *always* had issues with using your Gift but—'

'I don't have issues with it any more,' I said.

Geri raised her eyebrows. 'Well, good, then—'

'Then nothing. I didn't want to be able to mind-read,' I said. 'But as I can, I plan to use it to help people.'

'But that's what the Medusa Project *does*,' Geri insisted. 'And you don't have a choice about being part of the project, you know that. You can't leave.'

'I'm not saying I want to leave,' I said. 'I'm saying I want to choose who I go after and who I don't. I want it to be *my* choice, not yours. And I want proper attack and defence training. Every day.'

Geri glanced at the others, clearly hoping for some support. I looked at them as well. Nico nodded at me. Dylan, too. A small smile crept round Ketty's mouth.

'But, Ed dear, you're in no position to decide which criminals need to be dealt with most urgently,' Geri said, sounding flustered. 'Or when and how to make best use of your special skills. None of you are.'

261

'Aren't we?' Nico folded his arms. 'Why not?'

Geri's mouth opened and closed again.

'Ed's right,' Dylan said, getting up off the bed. 'If we're in the Medusa Project, then it has to be *our* project. You can give us options, but *we* decide who we go after.'

Ketty smiled. 'Exactly.'

A lump lodged itself in my throat. I was prepared to go ahead on my own, but I couldn't deny how good it felt that the others were with me.

'This is ludicrous,' Geri blustered.

'You don't have a choice,' I said. 'If you lock us up then you can't use us. And if you send us out on a mission or to another camp or something, then we'll just run away. Well, *I* will.' I glanced at the others.

'We *all* will,' Ketty said.

Nico and Dylan nodded.

'You've obviously made your minds up.' Geri pursed her lips. 'Well, it's not as easy as all that. You'll see.'

She left. As she closed the door the others turned to me.

'Way to go, Mr Ethics.' Dylan laughed.

I looked from her to the others. There was a new respect in their eyes.

'Why didn't you say something before?' Ketty said. 'What you're suggesting is a brilliant idea.'

'Yeah – but you might have warned us you were going to get all assertive,' Nico said. 'We could have braced ourselves.'

I laughed. Then I remembered Luz. I wandered over to the bay window which stuck out at the end of the room.

It was good to have everyone's support but, in the end, I was still alone.

We all are.

I knew that now.

Dusk was settling over the crowded city. Lights came on, sending the grey walls of the local buildings into shadow. There was bustle everywhere, with the old and the new, ancient shacks and modern tower blocks all mixed in together. The window was shut, but you could just make out the muffled yells of street traders and the blaring of a million car horns.

'You can still have a laugh sometimes.' Dylan appeared beside me. 'Just because Luz's gone doesn't mean you're never going to enjoy yourself again.'

I raised my eyebrows at her. 'I thought *I* was supposed to be the mind-reader round here.'

She shrugged.

I glanced over my shoulder. Nico and Ketty were chatting, their heads close together, poring over the hotel's in-house movie list.

'Don't those two make you sick?' she said tartly. 'They're so freakin' loved-up all the time.'

I stared at her, suspiciously. How come Dylan was being all chatty with me all of a sudden? And then I saw that she was actually trying, in a very Dylan-ish way, to be friendly.

I grinned. 'Are you trying to bond with me, Dylan Fox?'

She grinned back. 'Don't flatter yourself. You're just the only one left in the room to talk to.'

She wandered off, into the bathroom. I turned back and looked out over the city again. More lights were switching on.

Luz meant 'light', I thought to myself.

I sighed. *God*, was absolutely everything from now on going to remind me of her?

Oh well, maybe there were worse things.

'Hey, Ed, come and watch this movie we've found,' Ketty called.

'Yeah, it's advertised as "the thinking person's werewolf movie",' Nico added. 'You'll love it.'

And, smiling, I turned away from the window and walked back across the room.